W9-ADX-941

THE KILLING ZONE

HARPER'S
MAGAZINE
PRESS

THE KILLING ZONE

A NOVEL BY

William Crawford Woods

A HARPER'S MAGAZINE PRESS BOOK

Published in Association with Harper & Row

New York and Evanston

"Harper's" *is the registered trademark of*
Harper & Row, Publishers, Inc.

For

William Riddick Crawford

Lieutenant Colonel of Airborne Infantry

U.S. Army

K.I.A.

Luzon, P.I.

February 6, 1945

ACKNOWLEDGMENTS

This is a work of fiction. Its prototypes do exist outside its pages but do not live within them. I made this novel, but several people made the circumstances of its creation, and I would like to thank at least a few of them here. My specific literary debt is to Joseph Whitehill, whose initial interest and support opened the necessary doors for me; to Candida Donadio, who stood behind all of them; and to Herman Gollob, who thought I had news fit to print.

In a more general way, I was helped through the time of the book's design by a number of others—chief among whom were John and Constance Holland, Toby Thompson, my wife, Molly, my brother, Arthur, and my parents, Arthur R. and Louise C. Woods, whose full and free support has always been undoubted and unfailing.

The computer in the book was designed by Constance Holland, who was gracious with her time, generous with her information, and patient in correcting my use of it. If the machine works, it's hers. If it doesn't, it's mine.

W.C.W.

Say a prayer for the common foot soldier.
                        —Mick Jagger, "Salt of the Earth"

Do younger nations always win wars?
They are apt to for a time.
Then what happens?
They become older nations.
                        —Ernest Hemingway, *A Farewell to Arms*

Thus they determined at hazard of their lives to be honorably avenged, and to leave the rest; and on the battlefield, their feet stood fast, and in an instant, they passed away from the scene, not of their fear, but of their glory. Methinks that a death such as theirs has been gives the true measure of a man's worth; it may be the first revelation of his virtues, but it is at any rate their final seal.
                        —Thucydides, *The Peloponnesian War*

ONE

ONE DAY a young officer came to the company, came to command. The company had no executive officer. It had been in the charge of its first sergeant during the days since its last commander's death: Captain Hillock, who had died of an attacking heart on the seventh hole of an easy course on a sunny day.

For First Sergeant Lawrence Melton, the officer's arrival further complicated a morning already shadowed by the interminable paper work of yet another death. A private of the company, being taken under guard from the company area to the post stockade to await court-martial for some small offense, had attempted to escape, had been shot and killed by the man marching slowly behind him. Melton knew no difficulty in picturing the scene: the prisoner in his fatigues and dusty boots, a silver glint of handcuffs against the olive drab, the boy behind in khaki with the brilliant white of his web belt bleached and pure in the climbing sun, the black butt of the service automatic massive under its holster flap. Men would wonder for many days why the soldier had started to run, they would speak of it softly in the darkness of the best part of the day—the ten minutes after taps—but Melton knew the reason. Probably the man already seemed to feel the shaming

3

clippers baring the blue surfaces of his skull, to know the weight of the unfitting new fatigues that wore no name, no rank, no mark of place or unit, nothing but the broad whitewashed P emblazoned on back and chest; cloth that would mold in salt against his skin in the summer hotness as he sank a nine-pound hammer into the corroding body of one of the rusted trucks on the mountain of metal in the stockade compound, the scrapping of which served as the prisoners' tragic long employment.

Perhaps some cell or section of the man's brain, some part of him avid for freedom above all else, had taken charge between one footstep and the next, had turned his humble plodding to a hungry run, all touch with sanity gone; with common sense. The logic that told him his offense was relatively little and his punishment likely to be correspondingly slight had disappeared in that moment. Behind him, the guard must have been shocked, and then perplexed, but acting all the time, drawing his pistol and shouting his command, firing—much to his own surprise—firing a shot into the air, and then finally in desperation aiming a round into the fleeing soldier's legs. Aiming a .45 is an approximate matter at best. The shot sent to cripple had killed instead. The soldier, the prisoner, had died looking for a freedom time would have bought him, with sweat and boredom and humiliation, but probably with little pain. Yet perhaps he had been wise after all. Perhaps he knew that in the Army there are no small offenses.

Melton looked away from the door, through whose aging screen, orange with rust, he had seen the officer walking up the gravel path, and turned again to the three neat stacks of forms centered on his desk before him. It was Saturday morning. The company clerk was standing in the kitchen of somebody's apartment in New York City, his head in the refrigerator, trying to make the freezer devour his hangover; so Melton had assembled these forms himself. He would fill them out himself, type them himself, himself sign for his dead commander these dispositions of his commander's dead man.

The officer knocked at the screen and opened the door with what must have been two hands and one motion. Melton looked up.

A pale punk kid to run my company, another ninety-day wonder —no, worse: one of the type they commission right off the street because they know something modern Army green needs to know. Not soldiering. Business, or science, or something to do with an office, or with machines you can't trust, machines you can't see past their faces, machines that just stay still and talk in numbers, computers.

That much had come down with the information from Battalion. The officer would be hand-carrying his records, of course, but Melton had managed a copy of his 201 file. Thomas Tallin Track, First Lieutenant, Ordnance Corps. Twenty-four years old. BS and MS in electrical engineering from the University of California. Master's thesis on some military application of information retrieval. ROTC commission deferred until after graduate school. Part-time programmer for Armed Resources Corporation—one of those ambiguous concerns that hide in the rolling countryside of Maryland and Virginia within fifteen minutes by chopper of the Pentagon; semisecret compounds where men in short-sleeved white voile shirts translate Defense Department contracts into Fortran and the other tongues of Babel, and learn from the shimmering surfaces of their machines how to move the elements of war in an ordered march across the chessboard of the earth.

Computers. *Generations* of them, like the generations of men.

Melton knew other machines, and trusted them. Land motor vehicles of all kinds, some airplanes, and three models of helicopter. Almost all weapons. Typewriters and most manner of plumbing and electricity. Levers and pulleys. Entrenching tools,

5

with which to dig slit trenches for yourself or graves for your dead. *Or graves for my dead,* Melton thought, standing to acknowledge the intruder. *My dead, yes, how possessive I become of them as time binds them tighter from me.* Old Sarge, hard-assed campaigner, professional soldier. Time binds them tighter. He often thought in alliteration; he found it elegant, but carefully banished it from the rough texture of his speech, holding it secret among his fellows as an artist with a pool cue may guard his art amid congeries of amateurs. Melton read books, did deep thinking on duty time and serious drinking off (for he knew of the wisdom trapped in grain), had a lot of reflective vices the Army had given him six stripes and a diamond despite and not because of. He had poet's hands and a seamed face that successfully laid claim to carrying more than his fifty-three years. But alcohol and decades of Army starches had left no pockets of fat on either his face or his figure. And he didn't hate college kids; he made them corporals.

But this college kid . . . Somebody had gotten to him before Melton and made him a first lieutenant and sent him to the company to get in Melton's way.

The young officer had paused uncertainly in the doorway of the orderly room, like a lost trainee, a two-day trooper from the reception center. Melton looked past him to the new red Corvette in the gravel drive, a car the color of a whore's lipstick, and, still gazing at the car, said, "Yes, sir?" expectantly, because it seemed as though the new commander were going to stand in the doorway forever.

The lieutenant, released, came on in. "First Sergeant Melton?" he asked, properly using the full title of rank. "I'm Track. I'm the new CO."

The sergeant offered his hand, a bit grandly. "Yes, sir; I'm Melton. Glad to see you. I'm afraid I'm about all the welcome there is, though," he added with a hint of reproach. "Battalion HQ said not to expect you before tomorrow night."

"Well, no sweat, sergeant. I'm on my way to New York after lunch. I won't be around officially until Monday reveille. I just thought maybe I could get a quick impromptu look at my company this way, if you've got time to show me around a bit."

Twenty-four. Melton would have said twenty-six, at least. The lieutenant's dark hair was shaved close against his skull like a Marine's in a movie about Marines. He wore glasses—not gray plastic issue, but teardrop-shaped steel-rimmed lenses poured thickly full of glass, behind which the young officer's eyes lay blue as a girl's. He had a pink face and a jaw like a fist and his body was small and halfway trim. His arms came slender and hairy out of the stiff short khaki sleeves, lined but not laced with muscle. His uniform—well, issue khaki never did hold a day's wear or last after morning in summer. Melton spent his own money on gabardine twill and permapress, and the new lieutenant looked to have been after one more morning than this poor cloth would give. Or maybe it was from riding around in that car with the top down, getting sun on forehead and forearms and wind creases in his clothes. Melton managed an unobserved glance at the officer's shoes. Like black glass.

With a familiarity that might have been premature but wasn't —his judgment in such matters was rarely less than precise—Melton eased his buttocks against the edge of the desk. *If you've got time.* He didn't. There was death on the green blotter.

"Well, I don't know, sir. There's not damn all to see. Most of the troops are on pass. It's the first they've had this cycle." He immediately disliked the defensiveness of the last.

"That's fine. I'd just like to look around the area—meet the cadre, if there're any about."

Melton had read that people purse their lips if they want to look thoughtful. He approximated the *moue*. "I don't think there's a damn soul in the company but me and the CQ and the CQ runner. And the KPs. And the KPs are in the kitchen."

7

"I know where the KPs are to be found, sergeant," Track said thinly.

Melton had pressed the thinnest hair too hard. "Beg pardon, sir," he said, a Kipling color sergeant. "Uh . . . could the lieutenant use a cup of coffee?"

"Thank you. Yes."

The first sergeant went to the thirty-cup urn atop a file cabinet and drew some coffee into one of the white porcelain mugs that ringed the urn. If Track didn't finish it, he would never see the brown circle of crust at the bottom. Melton filled his own china mug and carried them both back to the desk. He did not drink out of porcelain; it was like drinking out of a toilet bowl.

"Thanks, first sergeant."

Track had taken the folding chair by Melton's desk. Sitting, he looked even smaller, his uniform exploded into yet more wrinkles. But his brass, like his shoes, bore a high luster. Melton saw the silver bar on one collar shine like a wedding gift, the little round gold flaming bomb on the other wink in the sun from the open window like a yellow diamond in a candle's glow. Track followed his glance.

"Yeah, Ordnance. I think they dropped all the branch insignia into a hat and assigned me to the one they drew out. I guess I got an infantry company the same way."

"That's encouraging."

Track grinned at Melton, looking to engage a nerve of the other's honesty and humor. "I'm a computer man in real life, first sergeant. I know you've probably been in the Army longer than I've been alive, and I know you'll still be in it when I'm back pushing buttons on the outside. I know that first sergeants run companies and that young officers keep the hell out of their way if they want the job done right. Is that the way you see it?"

Melton shrugged.

8

"OK. I plan to let it pretty much be that way. You run the company and I sign the paper work. Right?"

"You don't even have to sign all the paper work," Melton said. He was not impressed by the officer's humble frankness, his air of concession and goodwill. An officer before he was a soldier. A follower appointed to command.

Track laughed. He spooned too much sugar into his coffee and poured too much cream and balanced the cup on his knee until it spilled a little and then he drank some off and then he put it on the desk. "I'd like to see my office."

"Yes, sir."

Melton unlocked a door adjoining the orderly room and threw the switch to the overhead fluorescent light inside the daylight-dim area beyond. The light swam and flickered, then billowed cold and dry against the bare walls. Like the orderly room, the company commander's office was chill and new. Pink linoleum tile and ash-gray cinder block, green metal furniture: the pastels of a mental ward. The large desk was clean and bare. Track glanced at it.

"All the drawers cleaned out?"

"Of course, sir."

"It's a damn shame about Captain Hillock," the young officer said at last. "Hell of a way to go. On a golf course."

"Well, he played a lot of golf," Melton said, "He probably didn't mind the spot." A fat-fed heart presenting its final bill; face down in the cool cropped grass; fingers curled around the murdering iron. "Did you know the captain?"

"No."

"He was very orderly. Easy to clean up after." Melton looked around the office. He knew its bareness made it seem cleaner than it was. There would surely be a very thin layer of—not even of dust, but of something finer and more elusive, left by emptiness

9

and passing, on all the surfaces of the room. He would have to have a couple of trainees in here to clean up on Sunday night.

Track opened the venetian blinds. Warm glass gave him a view of several thousand square feet of rocky brown dirt and a rectangular brick building three stories high, new raw red brick and white mortar studded with rows of metal-framed windows. Against all but one, venetian blinds lay folded, giving the barracks grim repose. Inside the one, the lumpy green figure of a trainee was visible, his hands pressing cheesecloth to the glass, swimming in vague circles, hunting dust.

"Well," Track offered, "I guess that young man wishes he'd caught that window earlier in the day."

"Yes, sir," Melton said.

"How long has the company been without a head?"

"The company has never been without a head."

"I beg your pardon, first sergeant. How long have you been running things?"

"Just over a week, sir."

"Everything up to date? All the training going through on schedule? No recycles?"

"Everything's squared away, sir," Melton said.

Track lowered himself into the swivel chair behind what was now his desk. He punched on the desk light and opened all the drawers. They gave a metallic clatter. All were empty.

"Is there a key to this desk, first?"

"Yes, sir."

"One key only? No duplicates?"

"One only."

"Would you leave it here for me before Monday morning?"

"Yes, sir."

"OK. And I want all the usual office supplies—in twice the usual quantity. Also some graph paper and a flow-chart pad."

10

"A what?"

"Never mind, I'll take care of that. And can you get hold of an electric typewriter, pica type?"

"I think so, sir."

"Will I need field gear Monday reveille?"

"Well, not really, lieutenant."

"OK. I'll wait till Monday to check it out, then." He paused and looked around the room. Pink and gray and green, all muted by the soft dead light. It was like seeing a wall through the eyes of a fish. "And maybe you can chase down some stuff to humanize this place a little bit?"

"Sir?"

"Christ, a carpet, some pictures, I don't know."

"I'll do what I can, lieutenant."

"OK." Track looked up. "Have a seat, sergeant, please."

Melton had been standing in the doorway. He leaned around into the orderly room and took his coffee from the top of a file cabinet and then sat in the chair by Track's desk.

"Cigarette?"

"Thank you, sir." Menthol filter twenty millimeters too long. Melton accepted a light.

"What keeps you on post Saturday morning, first?"

"A dead thief," Melton said. "Well, he may have been a thief. He was AWOL, anyway, when they got him."

"Dead?"

"Sir?"

"Dead, did you say?"

"Yes, sir. A trainee in Cox's—Sergeant Cox's—platoon. They think he stole some money from a locker."

"That's a low form of barracks life," Track commented, "a snake." He said it as though he had read it on a poster in a provost marshal's office.

11

"Anyway, he cut out. They brought him back. Sergeant Cox brought him back himself. A guard was taking him to the stockade this morning when the crazy sonofabitch broke and ran."

"So the guard *killed* him?"

"Well, didn't go to. But you know a .45."

"Jesus."

"Yeah. It's a hell of a thing to welcome you to the company with, sir," Melton offered, "but I've already handled most of the paper work on it. I'm going to have Reynolds—the company clerk—type a letter to the kid's parents Monday morning for your signature, but I don't think you'll catch any flack."

"What are you saying in the letter?"

"I don't know yet, exactly. Something that will add up to 'died in the line of duty,' I guess."

"Yeah, that's best. Will the body . . ." He trailed off delicately.

"That does present a problem," Melton admitted.

"OK. Now what other good news have you got for me?"

"That's the worst. It'll make waves in the company for a while, but we'll keep them busy, too busy to worry on it. Ultimately it might even prove . . . good for discipline."

"Maybe," Track said. He had been thrown a little away from center by the death of one of his men. One of Hillock's. Dead Hillock. One of Melton's. "What week of this cycle is the company in?"

"Monday starts the sixth."

"You got any AWOLs—live ones? Anybody in the hospital?"

"We've got eleven in the hospital, all URI. Only one gone long enough to be in danger of recycling. No AWOLs. That's one eighty-one present for duty, sir."

"What the hell is URI?"

"Upper respiratory infection," Melton said. "It's what the Army doctors are calling a lousy cold this year."

"In the summer?"

12

"Can be a bad time. The infection spreads damn fast."

"Isn't sixth week bivouac?"

"Ordinarily."

"But?"

"The captain's death fouled up the schedule a little bit. We'll get it all in."

"What about field problems?"

"One at the end of the cycle," Melton said. "Three days."

"Big show?"

"Well, it's brigade level. Be a couple of basic infantry problems."

"Against Aggressor forces and all that?"

"Far as I know, sir."

"Simulated air and artillery support?"

"No, sir, I doubt it. It's just planned for the brigade, with organic equipment. There'll be plenty of stuff on it coming down from HQ shortly, and I guess you could see Major Haslip any time."

"The brigade—the battalion commander?"

"Yes, sir."

"OK, good. That's the part of the training in which I'm most interested, frankly. I'm going to want to know a lot more about it. We'll go into it further sometime next week."

"As the lieutenant wishes," Melton answered. He waited for Track to tell him to knock off the third-person address, but the officer went on, "What about my cadre? What can you tell me about them?"

"I'd rather let you judge, lieutenant."

"I'd rather judge," Track returned, "but time is not very much on our side, don't you agree? I have two weeks in which to finish a job of turning out combat infantrymen, a job somebody else started. Even more than usually, that puts the burden on my cadre—and on my first sergeant."

13

Melton permitted himself to indicate with a just audible sigh that he didn't have to be told where the burden was. "Well, you've got four good platoon sergeants, sir: three staff and a hard-stripe E-5 draftee, damn good man." That was Cox, whose work Melton had watched closely, and with increasing approval, for some months; approval less for his methods than for his manner, his swift dry professionalism that seemed to indicate he drew power from a central philosophy of his art not far removed from Melton's own. "Their people, the corporals and so on—I don't know all of them personally, but the platoon NCOs think they do a solid job. You've got a damn fine field first—Sfc Sherman. The other people are satisfactory. The supply people . . . Specialist Reynolds, the company clerk . . ." Melton stopped. The young officer was asking to be supplied free with images of his men that he would, after all, have to assemble for himself, whatever the time limit. Melton knew the capacities of the company cadre far more closely than he chose to indicate; but his reticence was not a perverse attempt to hamper Track in the CO's new and exacting work. It came rather from the knowledge that nothing Track could be told about a man would give him the same feel that he could get from working with him, from digging out the hints of weakness, power and nuance for himself.

"Who's the weak link?" Track wanted to know. "I don't mean who stays in the sack too long in the morning or who gets drunk at night. I mean who's the man in whom command might become too diffuse . . . who might let things fall apart."

Melton noticed with a formal inward smile that the officer had hesitated after pronouncing *diffuse*; he clearly feared he might have gone beyond the first sergeant's powers of vocabulary. Then his amusement, as it dwelled upon the unintentional slight, turned to a mild irritation, the irritation to a milder arrogance. "I don't know of any. And if I don't know of any, sir, there isn't one."

Track looked at him. There was a thin mist of red over his blue

14

eyes, under the lenses of his glasses. "I take that for granted, first sergeant."

Melton did not reply.

"When is reveille formation?"

"Monday? First call at 0500, formation at 0530, sir."

"What's the day's program?"

"Classes in the morning, drill and hand-to-hand after chow. Short march to first-aid training after that."

Now, men, don't let your buddy look at his wound while you're dressing it, and don't say, "Oh, Jesus," and start to puke when you see it, 'cause you'll just get him more upset, right?

"What classes?"

"Map reading and a refresher on the Code of Conduct, I think. Have to check my schedule to be sure."

"Good enough. Leave a copy of the training schedule for the rest of the cycle on my desk, will you? For Monday: run the day as planned. I'll speak to the company at the noon chow formation. I'll see the cadre in my office at 1300 sharp—that's just the platoon sergeants and you and the field first."

"All right, sir."

"I suppose the squad leaders and platoon guides can keep tabs on the troops for half an hour."

"Sure. Surely." *Sharp.* Track, if he became a good officer, would learn the things you don't have to say. "1300" *meant* 1300 sharp. Track would learn to give up tautological qualifiers.

The officer looked at his wrist. He was wearing one of those ten-dollar watches that have two dials and three hands and run at sixty fathoms or five atmospheres, watches you buy through an ad on the back of the sports page of the Sunday *New York Times.* "Well, I'm on my way. Party in town tonight." He shot the first sergeant a smile. Melton reflected that it looked like it was supposed to be what you call a winning smile.

Track stood up, and Melton stood with him.

15

"Don't trouble, first, I can find the door. One more thing." He indicated a wall of his office that was lined with empty gray steel bookshelves and green filing cabinets. "When you have them bring the office supplies in, have them cart some of that furniture out. I want a piece of that wall. I'm putting a computer in it."

"As you say, sir."

Over twenty years, Melton had served under commanding officers of personal whims so varied that they had long since ceased to amaze him. A captain at Fort Riley, Kansas, who had kept in his office an old cavalry saddle which had to be saddle-soaped daily by the detail that came in to scrub the floors. A captain on Okinawa who had a loaded BAR hanging on his wall. A major at Fort Devens, Massachusetts, with a pet baby alligator whose stomach had to be cleaned with a toothbrush. Not to mention officers who acquired elegant nervous mannerisms in combat and retained a style defined by that daily pressure. If Lieutenant Track wanted to play with a computer, it would turn that much more control of the company over to the man who was meant by the traditions of fate to do the job.

At the screen door, Track shook Melton's hand. Melton felt as though he were getting the secret grip of a small Midwestern fraternity. "Thanks for your time, first. See you Monday."

It was close to noon. The summer sun at zenith had left a layer of burn on the metal of the new CO's Corvette; Melton watched him open the low door gingerly and settle with squirms of dismay into the heated vinyl bucket behind the wheel. He departed modestly, all gravel quiet under the wide tires and the deep crumble of the motor. Melton could hear a faint din begin to pour from the car radio, rock music, loud and complex. Melton did not like much music—he liked it perhaps the way most men like poetry: one or two poems—and he very much disliked this music. It still seemed to him to bear a class distinction; it was not the sort of music an officer should be listening to.

The first sergeant refilled his cup and returned to his desk. He moved the stacks of half-completed forms neatly to one side, and set before himself a pad of ruled paper. *Dear Mr. and Mrs. Mateland.* This would follow the official notification; the tone needed to be personal and concerned. *It is with deep regret that I write you now to express my sympathy.* It is with deep sympathy that I write you now to express my regret. *As your son's commanding officer* . . .

Melton watched the slide snapping on the .45, saw the fat gold balls of the spent shells hop free of the cylinder, above the bucking motion of the pistol. A bullet for the legs becoming the artless carver of the backbone. The guard shocked by ritual murder under the eyes of the sun.

. . . *becoming a fine soldier. This tragic accident was in effect a battlefield death, though it cannot be so recognized or so rewarded, for it was truly a part of the toll soldiers pay for the land's defense, whether in combat or garrison, the jungle or the drill field. My cadre join me* . . .

Why, Mother America, I'd give him a DSC if I got one in change at the PX, indeed I would.

My cadre join me . . .

A thief's accidental destruction to be condoled by a commander who never commanded him. Melton struggled with his letter. Like many men who own a single great expertise, he prided himself on the grace with which he could perform chores alien to his central power. He took the best part of the afternoon finishing the letter, returning to it after lunch, leaving it only in time to complete the official forms before happy hour started at the NCO Club. Before he went home, Melton would drink moderately, until his mind had taken his impressions of Lieutenant Track through all possible swings and swims and jumps and connections, until he knew his new CO quite well, his new young officer who had come in the morning and driven away at noon. Melton's eyes had followed the

17

red car down the company street, watching the sun wink hotly off steel and enamel, off the silver bar on the gold-piped garrison cap Track had crushed against his skull in an effort which, searching for a jaunty air, had yielded only a careless appearance.

TWO

"ALL RIGHT, you people, listen up," Sergeant Cox said, but Private Pendleton, for one, wasn't listening. He was fair-haired, sallow-faced, overweight, and his lungs were full of garbage. He was wondering when he could get his ass back into the hospital, where he had spent four sleepy peaceful days earlier in the cycle with a fever he had fought to catch and a cough he kept alive by coughing. He was also wondering whether mail call would bring him a pair of stockings from his girl, two fine sweet nets of soiled nylon gaped with runs, female cloth he could press against his face in the hours of dark to fill himself with female salts and sweats. *Honey,* he had scribbled in his last hasty note, *one of the guys in the squad showed me how you can get a terrific spit polish on your boots by buffing them with a stocking. I know it sounds strange, but it works. The next time you get a run, could you send me the rejects?* And that was true: but Pendleton, who was usually too exhausted to be horny but too filled with civilian dreams to forget the strained quartets of flesh, knew that he would cap one stocking in his Kiwi and save the other for gamy secret joys. He hoped his girl wouldn't wash the stockings before she sent them.

He pressed the back of his right hand hard into the palm of

21

his left and tensed the muscles of his calves and thighs: part of the endless search for a way to relax at parade rest.

"Ahright, at ease," Cox said. "Listen up, goddammit," again, although the forty-five men—ringed in a lacy triple circle around him where he stood six feet above them on the green wooden platform, arms loose by his sides in emulation of the canvas dummy that hung silent in its frame behind him—though they had given no outward or visible sign of doing anything else. "Give me each and every young ear, because this shit I'm gonna tell you is gonna save your life, and even if you don't want your life, Uncle does, so listen to this good shit." The sergeant's voice was searching for urgency in the taxing terrain of a record endlessly replayed. "Now this is refresher shit, right? You had all this shit in basic, but then you went home for two weeks and pretended to yourselves that you'd never heard of the Army, you pretended to yourselves that the only hand-to-hand you needed was what you got from your girl when she grabbed hold of your joint and milked it like a puppy with a bone—*You!*"

"Yes, sergeant?"

"You got a girl back home, soldier?"

"Yes, sergeant."

"Does she do it all six ways?"

"Yes, sergeant."

"Bet you wish you were back there with her."

"No, I'd rather be here, sergeant."

"That's good. Because you *are* here." Cox paused. "You people would all be a lot happier if you knew where you were."

"Up your ass looking for papaya," Pendleton muttered.

"Did you speak, Private Pendleton?"

"No, sergeant."

"You got a girl, private?"

"Yes, sergeant."

"How does she like it, young man?"

22

"Any way I give it to her."

Cox snorted contempt. "You don't even know which end is up, soldier. When she gets on her knees you probably start praying."

"Hey, Sergeant Cox," somebody yelled, "I got—"

"You got syph. No, you got dandruff. That's all. Now you men knock off the goddam chatter in there and listen up. You forgot everything already, didn't you? You went and forgot it, just like you'd never have to use it." He paused and let his voice drop expertly into a lower register, into the soft menace of sincerity. "But you will have to use it. A lot of you really will have to use it. You don't believe that now. You figure you might have to squeeze off a clip at some underbrush someday. You maybe even realize you might have to pull the trigger on a man you can see. What you stupid bastards still don't know is that the fine day is gonna dawn when you're standing there all by your lonesome and that clip in your rifle is full of nothing but air, and you, you dickheads"— affection came into his tone—"you've forgotten to put the bayonet on the mother, or else you've lost it somewhere in a crap game with a leg, and that little gook sonofabitch is three feet from your face with a hatchet in his hand, or some other kind of good shit to slash your balls off with, and people, that young man is gonna *kill* you, yes, unless you know how to do *this*—"

And Segeant Cox turned sharply, with a shockingly high hard short scream, and his body did two intricate and graceful dances, one from the waist down and one from the waist up, his hands flashed and chopped, he weaved, went under the absent blade, and there were two loud reports from the dusty dummy that hung in the wooden arch before him, two quick new grooves in the worn green canvas, one in the side of the neck, one on the spot where the sightless eyes would have been. Cox turned away. The dummy swung. The ropes that held it creaked. In the cold empty air of fall, the creaking of the dummy sounded through the rambling of

23

the dry curled leaves that wound in congress over the bare black floor of the forest.

"Now, men, that gook motherfucker, unlike your skillful selves, who know how to make that move, is *dead*, which is fine anyway, and best of all, from your point of view, which is bound to be a little selfish and egocentric, he's dead instead of *you*. Now. I'm going to walk through it, and if you've got any questions, ask 'em now, 'cause combat, when you're in combat, it'll be a little bit too late. OK. Now. Move out with the left foot and keep the right behind you, flat on the ground and dragging, gliding for balance. Guard your face with your left, as you were, with your right hand, and go for his eyes with your left—keep it straight fingers extended thumb parallel your fingers and get your fingers into his eyes, men, right into his eyes until you get some brain under your nails. Men, if you do that right," Cox said slowly, reverently, "you can rip his whole goddam face off, pull it right off his skull like it was a washcloth." Slowly Sergeant Cox ripped the faceless dummy's face off.

Pendleton avoided looking at Young, who was feigning parade rest at his left. Young was a High Church Episcopalian with a graduate degree in art history. He had expected to be sent to the Army Institute of Heraldry, but something had fallen through. If Pendleton and Young glanced at each other now, they might very well start to laugh. Cox would be less than pleased. Rip his face off. It would be all right once the platoon had begun to walk through the stages of this macabre ballet; the general hue would swallow their unhappy mirth, their educated humor at learning the warfare manners of jungle beasts.

They had become friends much earlier, choked by laughter under an arch of oiled steel, all raw rush and genial fury, boots digging asphalt, elbows in agony with the weapons' weight.

What is the spirit of the bayonet?

Kill!

Again!
Kill!
Again!
Kill!
I can't hear you goddammit! WHAT IS THE SPIRIT OF THE BAYO-
NET?
KILL!

. . . long thrust, parry and return to guard. Some of the men
did it elegantly, men who had learned grace in a sport and now
gave that grace to the sport of blood. Pendleton, looking at the
short span of steel on the end of his rifle, had not been able to
help thinking beyond the art of the bayonet fighter to the act of the
bayonet killer. Overhead, Phantom jets from the nearby field had
scattered through the flocks of morning cloud, ambassadors of air
war, mathematics of flame. Below, the draftees had held the
ancient pose.

Across the road from the training area (it was a parking lot;
they were learning to kill like cavemen in a place where the pizza
truck would stop that night), behind a mesh fence, stood a row
of NCO houses, trim brick boxes indistinguishable from any
stale subdivision in the land. Pendleton, his hands slippery on the
stock of the rifle, could see women moving in two of the yards,
hanging wash. Underwear, overcolored sport shirts, fatigues, a
cowboy suit. Behind the fence, directly across from him, three
children stood, two boys and a girl, all very small, their fingers
curled through the links of the mesh, watching.

Fix.

A company all fingers twisting scabbards up end.

Bayonets!

Up and down the line, a pattern of locks and clicks shy on the
ear, steel soft as silver shining in the light. *You'll notice this bayonet is not as long as the one you used to see John Wayne jam
onto his M-1 on the Late Show. That's because some clever*

bastard finally figured out you don't need two feet of blade to open a throat, Cox had said, and now he said, "All right"—and his voice was tired—"pair off and walk through it. Then you'll try it out on the dummy. And when you dickheads make your moves, I want to hear some *noise."*

Dropping green baseball caps beside shuffling black boots, the men of the platoon turned dusty figures toward each other. With cries plaintive and sere, they put their bodies through unaccustomed replicas of the sergeant's savage speed. *That little gook sonofabitch is three feet from your face with a hatchet in his hand.* Perhaps they were tired. Perhaps they could not see him. Their bodies moved like the bodies of musicians working under water.

Cox walked down from the platform and moved among them like a mortal man, watching, listening, saying little, pausing at times to correct with strange gentleness a stance or a stroke. Among the awkward bodies of the draftees, his slight figure took on a firm distinction. Under his rolled sleeves, the flesh of his arms seemed stacked on the bone like cordwood. His fatigues were faded to a greenish white and pressed into edges so sharp they called for a scabbard. His stripes and patches, all solid black, hung from his narrow shoulders with the weight of metal. The buckle of his belt was a square stamp of flawless brass. His boots seemed as soft as cloth and as bright as a razor coming to kill you.

Sergeant Cox walked up behind Pendleton and Young. He was in time to hear Pendleton say, "Fuck Babe Ruth—fuck FDR—Yankee dog, you die!" Pendleton flashed a hand toward Young's face, a caress. Cox hit him swiftly with the rear-stranglehold-and-takedown and stepped away, hands at his belt. Pendleton looked for wind, finally found a breath, sat up slightly. Cox stood before him, dry and without menace.

"Jesus Christ," Pendleton offered.

Motion and shout subsided around them. The other men were watching now. The platoon sergeant did not correct them. He

26

looked down at Pendleton, at the honorable uniform filled with indifferent flesh. Pendleton had never wanted to be a soldier. No doubt he was too highly educated to do the manual labor of war. If he had had a more useful college degree, he would have been made an officer, and Cox would be saluting that sallow skin under its braid and bars. Perhaps this boy would have been Cox's commanding officer, would have been Track.

"You think this is funny, young man?" the sergeant asked finally. "You think this is a funny exercise? You think it's a joke?"

"No, sir. No, sergeant."

"You want to laugh about it while you're Brilloing the heel marks off the dayroom floor all night tonight? You want to laugh about it while you're putting in eighteen hours in the kitchen in the consolidated mess?" A consolidated mess feeds many companies. KP in its kitchen can be a circle of hell.

"No, sergeant."

"You'll see how fucking funny it is when you're out in the jungle saying 'Fuck Babe Ruth' and some gook fucker comes along and gives you a really good laugh."

Pendleton had figured out that, judging by the more entertaining shifts in American foreign policy over the last twenty years, the next brush war would be in Bolivia, in the mountains of Bolivia. He wondered if Bolivians were gooks. He said nothing.

"You hear me, boy?"

Cox was twenty, Pendleton twenty-three.

"Yes, sergeant."

"Yes, sergeant, yes, sergeant," Cox mimicked. "Get on your feet."

The trainee hesitated. "Are you going to knock me down again, sergeant?"

"Knock you down?" Cox asked incredulously. "You know a DI can't touch a trainee. I never touched you. This is just an exercise I'm showing you."

27

Several months ago, or so legend had it, a drill sergeant had been court-martialed for knocking a piece of cake out of a trainee's hand in a chow line. It might or might not have happened. Training posts abound with such stories, whose action is just enough removed in time to be untraceable. In the cycle before one's own, a trainee was killed when somebody mixed up a white phosphorous and a smoke grenade, killed when he lifted his face into a flight of machine gun bullets on the infiltration course, killed carelessly downrange on the firing line, killed in any of a dozen plausible killing zones. But always in the cycle before.

Pendleton got delicately to his feet.

"Sergeant Cox," he said finally, a space after each word marking his care in the choice of the next, "I don't want you to think I'm being disrespectful, because I'm really not . . . but can't you understand how strange it sounds to me to hear about ripping somebody's face off? I mean . . . I've been taught for the last twenty years to, ah *value* life . . . I guess. Now in just a few months I'm supposed to destroy it, to learn to destroy it."

It was an immodest claim to make for yourself; with horror, he realized that the speech—even if it sounded true to the sergeant— sounded false to him.

But Cox was not impressed, either by the soldier's proclamation or by the wise hush that had fallen over the other men. "Pendleton," he said, "I knew a guy once who was a Buddhist. Wouldn't eat meat because he didn't want to give pain to animals. I told him that plants felt pain, too, and he said, 'Yeah, but they don't scream as loud.'"

"I wouldn't have figured you for a college man, sergeant."

"Oh, I had a month or two. But listen, that's a pretty common thing to say, young man. Why don't you eat shit?"

Pendleton shrugged. "Fifty billion flies can't be wrong."

"Good. That's very good."

"Seriously, sergeant—"

28

"Seriously, that sounds like a personal problem to me, trooper," Cox said promptly. "That's what we got chaplains for. You get in touch with the chaplain, Pendleton, and he'll punch your card for you."

"Yes, sergeant."

"Be sure and make an appointment, now."

"Yes, sergeant."

"In the meantime, try to act like a soldier. I know it won't be easy, because you're not a soldier, you're a pussy. But try, Pendleton. Try for me. Try for Sergeant Cox."

"Yes, Sergeant Cox."

The platoon sergeant looked at Pendleton for another few seconds, then swung away. "Squad leaders, form up your squads. One, two, three, four, line-number order. Send 'em through the dummy."

The line formed and moved. Hands crashed into canvas, cries of murder went into the brown trees around the training circle. Cox stood at the base of the platform, rocking slightly on his heels, his whole small body attentive, face raised to watch his running men. His eyes were as blue as the eyes of an Appalachian nun who uses carpet beaters on retarded children. His curly hair was cropped into a cap of sand. "I'll give a case of Black Label to any man who knocks that fucker clean off its hinges!" Several weeks ago, that offer had actually cost Cox a case of beer; he was not sorry. A short poem came into his mind as he watched his people:

> If I ever really learn karate
> Will I have to give up jerking off?

Rain had begun to fall as Pendleton and Young came out of the vast pink steaming mess hall. Its black fathering clouds were built high above the line of twilight, red and sullen behind the

29

long rows of lighted barracks. The men's olive fatigues turned black in the spots where the drops of water hit them. Pendleton had bought a newspaper from the little boy who sold them on the mess hall steps; he held it folded above his head for a minute and then let it drop.

"You might as well use it for that," Young said sourly. "You won't have time to read it tonight."

"Oh, yes, the party, the party. Are you invited too?" Pendleton stopped and took a thin cigar with a cherry-flavored wooden tip from the deep pocket of his shirt. He cupped a flare of butane against the light wind. "Don't walk fast, man, fuck the rain, this is the best part of the day. Let's go to the PX."

"Cox catches you at the PX you'll still be partying after everybody else has gone to bed," Young said.

Pendleton shrugged. "I got fire watch tonight anyway."

"When?"

"Two to three."

"Oh, Jesus, that's a beautiful time. You won't be worth a shit tomorrow."

"I won't be worth a shit until the day I hang my monkey suit in mothballs. Come on, let's go"

It was the best part of the day. For as much as twenty minutes he could be by himself, graced for those minutes with the illusion that there was no one he was responsible to. Granted there was little he could do, few places he could go. But he could briefly be at the center of his own time.

"Willet looked like he was about to pass out, didn't he?"

"His fault for getting there late this morning. Last man gets pots and pans," Pendleton intoned.

"Just because you've got good habits."

Pendleton did have a good habit where KP was concerned. He would have the CQ wake him just past three A.M. so he could get to the mess hall first and be outside man. The dull misery of rising then, of plunging and staggering through the motions of shower and shave, were worth going through to be spared eighteen hours inside the kitchen, faint with heat, hands turning sour under the endless thrust of gritty water. The outside man just swept up and watched the garbage and cleaned the mops and hosed down the concrete platform the trash trucks backed up to and kept the area in good police. Most of all, he was outside.

It was a good, responsible semper-fi military habit. That made Pendleton uneasy.

"Anyway, he misses out on tonight," Young said.

"What?"

"Willet. He won't have to help with the GI party."

That was true. And he wouldn't, either. When you have almost no rights, you expend an unbelievable amount of energy guarding those you do have.

"Last time I had KP I had to clean the ovens," Pendleton mused. "You know those ovens never get entirely cooled, not even if they haven't been used for a couple of days? You have to lie on your back inside them in the grease and scrub the top until little flakes of crud fall all over you."

"I'm glad you mentioned that," Young said. "I was thinking about re-upping, but now I ain't so sure."

"Oh, Jesus," Pendleton exclaimed, "don't let me stand in your way. Matter of fact, I was about to urge you to see your post re-enlistment NCO at your earliest opportunity. There's a bonus for certain MOS-qualified personnel, you know."

"Does that include light weapons infantry?"

"Why, mercy, yes!"

"And there's always the fifty-cent movies."

"Ten-cent beer."

"Travel, training, adventure."

"All medical expenses paid."

"Christ, it sounds wonderful. Put me down for twenty."

31

"Right. Go down for twenty."

The PX served only that area of the post. It was not the main PX, and it was very small; but it was superbly well equipped with things no one in his right mind would want: huge cardboard vats of trouser blousers, rank on rank of black paste boot polish, orange-backed brushes, baskets of wood and wire coat hangers, folded piles of white laundry bags, plastic soap dishes, shower thongs, stacks of underwear. Fluorescent bulbs washed the goods with pale files of light.

Pendleton bought six Baby Ruths.

"Jesus Christ," Young said, "are you making up a Care package for the folks back home, or what?"

"I didn't eat chow. I can't eat that garbage."

"It's not that bad."

"No—I know. Maybe it's just the feel of it, eating in the mess hall. It's such a huge deception, plastic flowers on the table, all that. It makes the food seem worse than it is."

"Man, that's altogether spiritual. I didn't know you were such a sensitive guy."

"I'm not. But when you start falsifying the nature of your food, you don't know what kind of trouble you'll end up with."

"You astonish me. Say on."

Pendleton had bought a pack of new cigarettes at the PX: multiple-filtered, air-vented, nicotine-robbed, charcoal-choked new cigarettes. He opened the pack, lighted one, took a drag, and tossed the pack and the lighted cigarette into a Dempster Dumpster.

"OK," he said. "See how much sense this makes to you: separated from the cities—but only by charity an item of the country —there are eating places, I won't call them restaurants, near the Pentagon. I mean, they're all over the fucking landscape, but I'm thinking of the ones near the Pentagon. Lot of the time these places are stuck in the middle of weird instant communities of

32

old-fashioned modern brick townhouses that have their own little man-made lakes and gas lamps outside every door."

"Don't let me stop you."

"Or else they're in shopping centers. Man, in America today, shopping centers exist in profusion in deserts, forests, wildernesses. Anyway. The eating places are called things like King's Contrivance or Lance and Tankard or Royal Arms, and they're always air-conditioned, dimly lighted, paneled in plastic molded like oak. The menus are often elaborate, but the food is always bad."

"Zap me."

"Here it is: it doesn't matter, because if you work for the Pentagon, you lose your ability to recognize bad food."

"Are Baby Ruths good food?" Young asked.

They came into the barracks out of the stopping rain and went up to their floor. They had to walk around men already on their knees on the stairway digging fretfully at black heel marks on the linoleum with frayed patches of steel wool.

They went into their room, and Pendleton buried the four uneaten candy bars in the bottom of his locker. They took off their boots and shirts.

It was an eight-man room—modern, well heated, almost comfortable compared to the old forty-man-bay wooden barracks. But its venetian blinds were landing fields for intolerable dust, its spacious lockers trapped phalanxes of grime, its linoleum floors picked up scuffs more readily than a magnet raises iron, its walls of pastel cinder block always seemed sunk in an unclean film.

By tomorrow morning at 0600, this room—and the dozens like it, and the halls and stairs that connected them, and the latrines that flanked them, and the dayroom below them, where no one was ever allowed to go during the day, or for any purpose except to clean it during the night—all these places would have to be standing tall.

33

"Well, how do you want to work this?" Young asked faintly.

"I don't give a shit who does what," one of the other men said, "but somebody better go steal a buffer now, else we'll be looking for one in the morning."

"Don't forget to put a towel over it," somebody else said, "or there'll be scratches in the wax."

"Isn't it grand for grown men to be occupied with these questions?" Pendleton asked. He picked up a tuft of steel wool and a clean butt can full of water and sat down wearily on the floor by his bunk. He found a little nest of black heel marks and began rubbing at them slowly and gently.

"When you empty that can out," Young said, "make sure you don't leave water marks in the basin." He turned on his tiny transistor radio, and an instantaneous hood of hard rock sprang from it.

They began their work at quarter after six in the evening. Shortly before two in the morning, they were finished. Sergeant Cox walked through the corridor and latrine they were responsible for, and then through the room. He looked at everything, said nothing, and walked out again.

"That's that," Young said.

"There isn't even any goddam point in my going to bed," Pendleton said bitterly.

"Two hours sleep is all any man needs," Young said. "You'll know it was all worth it in the morning when the lieutenant steps in front of you and says, 'Where're you from, son?' in a rich, fatherly voice."

"As if he were really going to be here. Melton'll inspect us, like always."

"My God, look," someone said softly. A mote of dust, translucent, was moving slowly across the floor as though alive. "Here comes dirt."

34

They all watched the dirt march slowly out the door. It was almost two o'clock, so Pendleton followed it.

"Fire watch, do your duty," someone else said. "If this concrete blockhouse catches fire, be sure to let me know."

"Jump up and bite my ass," Pendleton said.

For a long time, he leaned against the wall in the dimly lit corridor. The floor under his feet, in their thick black combat-boot socks, was soft, and shone with a rich gloss in either direction, as far as he could see. Lights began to click off under the closed doors of the rooms, but another half hour passed before there was full darkness and the partial silence of the lightly sleeping company.

Pendleton, alone in the darkness, found himself running through his mind a movie of Sergeant Cox's superb ballet of murder at training that afternoon. He had not chosen to think of it, and he did not make it welcome. But the darkness had summoned it as a pentagram draws the devil. Yes, Pendleton thought, Cox is the devil. And then he knew unhappily that Cox was merely a man who did a terrible thing so well that the thing had beauty; that his own humanistic scorn was as much a shame of arts unmastered as a fear of crimes despised.

So he made himself think about his girl.

Pendleton went into the latrine and into a booth and locked the door. He was exhausted and irritable, but he was mostly bored, with that boredom which is a mask for dread. He lowered his fatigue pants and his shorts, leaned against the door and took hold of his penis, foolishly pleased—as always—to find it where he had left it. When he was done, he scraped the lake of semen from his palm into the wider bay of the toilet bowl; he pulled his pants up and replaced his boots to make them tighter and more comfortable. He squared away his gigline and glanced at his wrist. There were still more than twenty minutes left in the hour he had

35

to stand fire watch. He went back into the deserted dim corridor, came to attention, and began to march noiselessly down to the other end of the barracks. When he reached the far wall, he came to attention again six inches from the blank pink cinder block, executed a precise about-face, and began to march in the other direction.

THREE

IN ACTUALITY, Track had an empty wall for a good many weeks. His first cycle had come and gone without further large mishap, his second was well under way when the terminal was installed. He had mentioned the computer to Melton at their first meeting in order to keep the sergeant's anticipation keyed to a useful pitch, in order to define one boundary of the control they would share over the company.

Track had not come into the Army harmlessly, or unbefriended. In California, at Armed Resources, even—it may be—at the Pentagon, he had coreligionists to work over the road ahead; despite which, there was no possibility of his arriving at the post one weekend and having his matrix ready the next.

Monday, Track settled in at the company. Melton had accomplished all that he had asked. His office was shining; supplies littered its shelves; a wine-colored rectangle of rug masked the linoleum before his desk; around the walls hung illustrated posters expounding the Code of Conduct.

I AM AN AMERICAN FIGHTING MAN. I SERVE IN THE FORCES WHICH GUARD MY COUNTRY AND OUR WAY OF LIFE. I AM PREPARED TO GIVE MY LIFE IN THEIR DEFENSE.

There was an American flag and an Army flag flanking the chair behind the desk. The commander's name plate rested in front of his beige blotter.

THOMAS TALLIN TRACK
1ST LT.   ORD.

Track met his cadre that afternoon: Sherman, the sergeant first class who was his field first, a tall heavy man of forty who carried himself like someone proud of a large and often-tapped capacity for violence; Staff Sergeant Disenhaus, platoon sergeant of the first platoon, an overweight German with narrow Nazi eyes: *I myself hate the methods of the Gestapo, but if you will not answer my questions* . . . ; Staff Sergeant Rellin, second, a black soldier haloed with the sure quiet wisdom of street breeding refined by jungle war; Iacone, third, expressionless and remote; William Robert Cox, the E-5 draftee in charge of the fourth. All the men save Cox were veterans of Vietnam; Sherman of Vietnam and Korea; Melton of Vietnam and Korea and the Second World War.

Track spoke to them briefly, in somewhat the way he had spoken with Melton two days before. It is unlikely that any of them were impressed, though all were polite, save Cox, who kept staring out the window at his platoon, which was doing calisthenics under the direction of the platoon guide on the field in front of the barracks. Their shouted numbers—*You will count the cadence, I will count the repetitions*—came thinly through the glass as Track talked. Want you to know that I hear you've been doing good work. Want you to keep it that way. A tough time for all of us for a while. A good company. Work together. My door is always open. Pride. Highest possible. Don't hesitate. Get to know you all.

After they had gone, the lieutenant sat studying their 201 files, waiting for it to be time for him to see Major Haslip. He had

40

called the battalion commander's office Saturday and made the appointment. It was the first step.

He began with Melton.

The first sergeant had been in the Army since 1937, with a break of two years after the Second World War when he had tried his hand in small-business management as a civilian. He had taken a reduction to come back in, but was wearing six stripes again a year later. He had done time in Armor and in AG, but for the most part it had been year after year—decade after decade—of crossed rifles and robin's-egg blue. He had served in Europe in World War II, coming out of it with wounds and rank and ribbons and the promise of a commission he hadn't wanted.

He had been in combat again in Korea, where, during the worst days after the Inchon landings, he had assumed command of a critically decimated company after all its officers were killed, held an untenable position for several days of the most savage hand-to-hand fighting, and relinquished it only when his superiors were advised that the hill was "politically unsafe." Melton had led his company—now numbering seventeen men—down without demur. Several of the men reported that the sergeant had saved their lives; had repeatedly exposed himself to the enemy guns, moving from place to place to supply new firepower for wounded and exhausted men; had engaged the Chinese suicide charges again and again with rifle butt and bayonet. Melton was nominated for, but finally did not receive, the Congressional Medal of Honor.

He added a second star to his CIB in Vietnam.

Track finished with the first sergeant's papers and sat for a few minutes, thinking. Then he went slowly through the files of the platoon sergeants.

He lingered longest over Sergeant Cox's records. The man's attitude during the briefing—his evident boredom, his unconcealed eagerness to return to the ritual-ridden daily tasks of his platoon—had irritated the lieutenant, not least because Cox had

41

managed to make himself just attentive enough to escape rebuke. Having thus singled himself out as someone either provisionally discourteous or actually superior, he had unwittingly signaled his commanding officer to make a search for the evidence either way. His 201 was the obvious place to begin.

The record offered at best an ambiguous satisfaction: Cox simply had not been in the Army long enough to accumulate the plaudits he seemed so clearly destined for. He had no combat experience—in fact, no overseas service—and his awards were limited to the National Defense Medal (Track's own only ribbon: "blue for the seas never crossed, red for the blood never shed, yellow for the reason why"; you got to pull one out of the barrel and take it home after basic), the Good Conduct Medal, jump wings, and an Expert designation on a variety of weapons. No: there was also the unadorned blue rectangle of the Expert Infantry Badge. Track thought sourly that the sergeant would no doubt be delighted to give a length of limb, bone or brain, a quart or two of blood to put a wreath around it.

In other respects, his record was striking. His promotions had been extremely fast: E-2 out of basic, Pfc two months later, Sp4 with waivers a month after that, sergeant E-5 within eight months of entering the Army. And he had several solid service schools: leadership, airborne, jungle warfare. It was pretty clear what he had wanted. But drill sergeant's school came into the picture, then assignment to a BCT brigade, and then assignment to this company. There followed a neat stack of requests for transfer to a combat unit, with a corresponding series of rejections signed by Captain Hillock, all bearing basically the same message—Cox was simply too damn good at his job of training to be wasted in the job he trained men for.

Track crushed his clammy minted cigarette into a worn tin ashtray that bore the faded legend "YOUR FLAG—YOUR FUTURE—GO ARMY," and looked swiftly through the sergeant's medical

42

records, which gave a story of good health marred only by a toothache the previous winter and a slight cold the same month. There were no other entries, no—for example—psychiatric notes. Track realized that, for some reason, he had been hoping to find such.

He looked next at the forms dealing with education. Cox had had less than one year of college, at a small liberal arts school in the Midwest. Track knew of the school and was surprised. It was tough, liberal, aggressively classical. He was not surprised that Cox had left to join the Army, but rather that he had chosen that college to begin with. Something failed to jibe.

The sergeant's grades had been passably good. He had not flunked out; he had simply left. Since then, other than the service schools, he had completed a USAFI course in political science.

The only other things of interest in the 201 file were several letters of commendation and one of reprimand. Track read them all carefully.

The letters of commendation were from the commanders of each of the service schools, and from Captain Hillock himself. They praised, mechanically, the young sergeant's perseverance, initiative, high accomplishment, aggressiveness, tenacity, job skills —and on and on, a dreary list of military virtues. Lacking all personal note, and much detail, they made surprisingly boring reading. But lists of virtues always do.

The letter of reprimand was from Captain Hillock. There was a feeling of reluctance in it, as though pressure had come from somewhere above him to write it, to give a hint of character to an otherwise blandly faultless record. Cox had evidently gone a little far in his disciplining of a trainee—apparently he had imposed an excessive punishment or required a too strenuous repetition of a duty—the evasiveness of the letter made it hard to tell exactly what the matter had been. *You are reminded that an excess of zeal can sometimes be as grave a fault as too much indulgence,*

43

and that the soldier in this instance may have been performing to the limit of his capabilities. In future, you will—

Track suspected that, in future, Cox would continue pushing people beyond the limit of their capabilities. Beyond the limit of what they thought were their capabilities.

He lighted another green-flavored cigarette and shoveled the litter of papers back into their manila folder. Cox was at least intriguing. He had come out of a nondescript background (in the precise sense that nowhere along the line had anybody in Personnel seen fit to give a description of it) into a hothouse of classical sciences, philosophies and literatures, where he had been passingly if briefly successful, and then moved swiftly into the world of the Army, where he had succeeded brilliantly, but always on the periphery of the Army's true purpose. He was highly trained, and obviously highly motivated, as they say, as a combat platoon leader; yet he seemed to have been trapped in a perpetual cycle of training. He was clearly officer material, and must have been pressured about that from the beginning, but there was nothing in his records to indicate that he had even considered appointment to OCS. He was extremely young and lacking in experience, but gave every indication of being a superlative soldier in a classic mold.

So there it was. There could be no doubt that there was at least one man on the company staff naturally fitted to give a certain special scope to the experiment Track was about to begin.

As the lieutenant put the records away, another odd omission from the 201 crossed his mind. Cox had a wife. But he had never, at any time, requested leave.

When the time for the meeting came, Track drove slowly through the post, his skin feeling raw and somehow infantile under his new fatigues. At an intersection, road guards fell in to block him, rendered salutes, locked into parade rest before the files that passed behind them: a company returning from a march, its guidon limp in the hot wall of air and the slow step, its people turned to personnel, diminished by their packs and weapons. Even the cadre, moving on the fringes, blue helmet liners nodding, seemed robbed of the energy to do more than walk like men where they should have marched like soldiers.

But now they were moving into the post again, headed for their own company area, where their pride would regain command. They had been at route step. Now orders snapped them into order, rifles straightened on shoulders raw with rubbings of cloth. Somewhere on the other side of the files an NCO chanted:

"First p'toon—count cadence delayed cadence count cadence COUNT!"

"One!" step step step "Two!" step step step "Three!" step step step "Four!" step step step "One!" step "Two!" step "Three!" step "Four!" step "One two three four! One two three four!"

"*Who are you?*"

The company shouted its name. Soon, Track thought, he would march his company through these streets, and they would look this proud, sound this proud. NCOs on the flank of the passing line saluted Track's car. In the weary wet hot center of the march, an old song began.

> Ain't no use in lookin down
> —*ain't no use in lookin down*
> Ain't no discharge on the ground
> —*ain't no discharge on the ground*
>
> Ain't no use in goin home
> —*ain't no use in goin home*
> Jody's got your gal and gone
> —*Jody's got your gal and gone*
>
> Sound off
> —*Sound off . . .*

It seemed to the young officer in the car that they were singing to him, that they were passing in review. Masked by the rising tan of dust, another platoon pounded by, its voice raised in raw contest with its brother.

> If I die in a combat zone
> —*honey, honey*
> If I die in a combat zone
> —*babe, babe*
> If I die in a combat zone
> Put me in a box and ship me home
> —*honey, baby, mine. . . .*

The rear guard moved by at last: running, panting, stumbling figures responding desperately to the ceaseless calling of the guides —*Close it up! Close it up!*—men who had to jog now through their own burning breathing because they had fallen back, walked too slowly earlier, because they had trailed into disorder at the ends and edges, as companies in motion invariably will—the inflexible justice of the long march.

The company passed. The last road guards, recalled, hurried back along the winding olive lines. The thin tongue of the guidon, white muskets on a field of blue, stood far above the fading voice of song. Dust settled like a mossy breath on the enamel of the lieutenant's car, muting the compound wax he had had applied for fifteen dollars that weekend in New York.

Major Haslip's office was a translation of Track's own, both smaller and more elegant. The battalion commander, knowing the purpose of the lieutenant's visit, had summoned the officer in charge of the post's computer system, a thin captain named Page whose eyes were faded to the color of the dim light of library stacks. Their trade their introduction, the junior officers talked readily about software, circuits and codes. Haslip talked about money.

"The rent on one of those terminals you want, lieutenant, might run more than seven hundred bucks a month, right—Captain Page? Right?"

Page nodded.

"Where do we get the authorization for that kind of money? This whole thing will have to go through the commanding general here and then DA and maybe DOD and Christ knows what-all. This is an infantry training post, lieutenant. All we want is for you to produce men who can shoot and salute, as I believe it was Black Jack Pershing said. I appreciate your initiative, but we don't have room for a Clausewitz, and we don't have seven hundred bucks a month lying around unwanted."

"The post has already got most of what I need, sir," Track said promptly. He did not add that he might be able to provide for the rest in a fashion more direct than through the slow crawl up the chain of command the battalion commander seemed wedded to. "A computer designed for multiprogramming and multipartition operations. It's a closed shop, so there's no way for somebody to screw up a remote shot with a hands-on run. You've got everything here. All I want is a piece of the action to plug into."

Captain Page glanced at him. Not only was Track swamping the major with jargon, he wasn't even troubling to keep the logic of his language truthful or entirely straight. But Track knew what he was doing; he was acting out of that peculiarly contemporary wisdom that tells us a speaker of one private language is likely to be impressed by a speech in another. As a career military officer, Haslip had spoken in tongues all of his professional life. To him, thickets of technical prose would sound like the voice of special competence.

Haslip turned to Page. "Captain, just what the hell does our computer do, anyway?"

"Well, it's the post's ear—and voice—in the Defense Communications Network, sir. Primary use is analysis and control of all nonorganic logistical problems, which are handled on a flexible basis, inasmuch as the matrix is directly operational on an indeterminate period of three hours out of the twenty-four."

Haslip said, "What?"

"Sir," said Track, "for three hours a day, your computer orders toilet paper and toothpaste for the troops. The other twenty-one, it sits on its ass." He lighted a cigarette.

"Is that true?" Haslip demanded of Page.

"Well, it's a gross oversimplification, sir."

"Just tell me whether or not it's true, captain."

"Yes, sir, it's true."

"Jesus Christ. That's a pretty light duty day. And just what is it you want, young man?"

"I want to get more mileage out of the thing, sir."

"How?"

"By getting appropriations for several more time-sharing terminals to be installed at the points on post where they would give maximum use. They'd be good in virtually any type of training. Each would have access to its own slice of the core, where memory banks holding all relevant information—"

"And you want one for yourself to play with."

"I don't think that's the best way to put it," Track said. He turned to Page. "Captain, are you familiar with a University of California monograph entitled 'Supervisory Programming Techniques for Small-Unit Actions'?"

"Of course."

"I wrote it."

"Sir," said Page, "if he wants a terminal, give him one."

That was not the end of the discussion; nor did Track hesitate to make the private arrangements his extramilitary contacts opened up; and by fall, the waiting space on his office wall was waiting no longer. The terminal was installed five weeks after the beginning of the company's new training cycle.

It was not an impressive object. First Sergeant Melton, who had innocently envisioned towers of metal disfigured by bursts of light and spinning blue reels of magnetic tape, gazed with some disdain at the modest tool his CO was looking over with interior but evident satisfaction. It resembled a telephone and a typewriter mounted in a narrow high desk.

"So this is where World War Three gets its marching orders," Melton remarked.

"This might be what keeps World War Three from happening," Track said.

"I'm all ears."

It was a politeness. Melton knew the young officer would be eager to talk about his new toy, and he felt benign toward Track that day. They were alone in the office. From the orderly room came the steady tapping of the company clerk's typewriter—Specialist Reynolds totting up the week's laundry list, or writing a letter to his girl.

"Well, look at the world first," Track said.

"I've had more appealing offers, sir."

"In twenty years—hell, less—computers will be able to model, in the smallest detail—You understand what I mean by model? Theory building?"

"Yes, lieutenant," Melton said patiently.

"Right; model in the very smallest detail any aspect of the status of the enemy, whoever's the enemy. I assume there will be an enemy in twenty years."

"Yes, sir, there'll be one."

"Politics, economics, the number of grains of rice on a farmer's dinner plate and the number of tines on the fork he eats them with."

"U-2s. Spy satellites."

"Yeah, sure. But I'm talking more about the virtually unlimited information we'll have on tap in the memory banks of computers. And, assuming the enemy's computers are the same generation, the same sophistication as ours—and they will be—he'll be able to do the same with us."

"A Mexican standoff," the first sergeant offered obligingly.

"And what's the result? On a global level, stalemate. Massive military assault with conventional weaponry is no longer an acceptable diplomatic method. Nuclear capability can't easily be translated into a meaningful threat in ordinary military terms. So what's the alternative?" Melton felt his own presence fade. Track was lecturing to a larger class. "Transference of power to another sphere. Manipulation of economies, even of ecology. Our computer tells us the bad guy has already had too much rain in his northern valleys, so we let it be known we'll salt his clouds for him even worse unless he toes the line for us somewhere ten thousand miles away. And he does the same to us. That's an oversimplification, of course, but not a hell of a big one."

"Sounds like science fiction."

"Good science fiction has always been reliable prophecy."

Despite the officer's classroom tone, Melton had become a little interested. "So war gets to be just a sort of game of comparisons between our pictures of each other. Between what our computers tell us."

"Precisely."

"Jesus."

"Computer matrices on both sides will cope—at incredible, literally unthinkable speed—with every relevant variable: past experience, available present data, coincident pressures, power plays at the top, sociological factors. If we need to know the color of a top official's wallpaper in order to decide whether to walk softly or breathe harder, the computer'll tell us."

50

"That all pretty much puts an infantryman out of work, don't it?"

"Hell, no," said Track. "It makes his work a lot clearer. But it might put the bomber boys next door out of work."

"Wouldn't it be possible for the thing to give you so damn much information you wouldn't know what to do?"

"Yes. It would. When that happens, you let it tell you what to do."

"I thought you could only get out of those things what you put into them."

"In twenty years' time, we'll have put everything into them."

"And that's what does it?" Melton asked, indicating the silent instrument against the wall.

"That's what talks to what does it." Track picked up the telephone. "I get at my hunk of the beast by dialing a private code and putting the receiver . . . here."

"You talk to it? In English?"

"No, no. This just lets me get at it. We talk back and forth on the keyboard."

"In English?"

"Not usually. It likes talking in numbers better."

"Why the code?"

"So I don't take a bite out of somebody else's piece of the machine. What happens is, I have my own partition, my own section of the core of the computer—the main storage area—with assigned input and output devices. That way a number of people can use the core simultaneously without getting in each other's way. In other words, I can be running a program from this office while somebody in Supply is putting in a request for bed sheets."

"What kind of program?"

Track shrugged.

"Sir," asked Melton, "just what the fuck you going to do with this thing?"

51

Track lighted one of his long cigarettes. "I'm going to try to prove a theory, sergeant, and at the same time improve the realism and effectiveness of our training." A chime of the pompous sounded deep within the line.

"How?"

"What's the purpose of infantry training?"

Melton was momentarily tempted to ask clemency from the Socratic method, but he took up his role dutifully. "Making soldiers."

"Making combat soldiers. And what's the best way to do that?"

"Simulate combat situations."

"OK. I've told you what computers are going to do to global warfare—"

"Eliminate it."

"Not eliminate it, exactly. Drastically change its terms. What I'm after is altogether different. I want to see just how useful computers can be in a more limited, and therefore more complex, situation. Not world war, but fluid small-unit action. There hasn't been a great deal of work done in that area."

"That's more complex?"

"Sure, in a way. Look at it like this. When you're dealing with enormous powers and forces, you can get by with relatively gross information on them. But say you want a computer to tell you *exactly* how best to lead a company, or even a platoon, foot by foot in a given combat situation. When it gets down to that, you've got to be able to deal not only with quantifiable variables— firepower and so on—but with qualitative things like morale." He paused. "Like courage."

Melton looked across the CO's desk. Track's gaze met his— youthful, confident, inflexible, unwise.

"I'm not sure a computer will help you too much on that one, sir."

"Don't bet against it."

Melton groped. "Yeah, but I thought—you know—they don't have emotions, right? Computers? They're not really like brains? Or minds?"

"Computers may be what finally tell us if the brain and the mind are the same thing, Larry," Track said, "but forget that for now. The point is, they *can* handle qualitative problems."

"How? If they only talk in numbers?"

"Through statistical analysis. Or any form available for reducing psychological data to logical form—mathematics. If you know how many troops had colds in September, you can figure roughly how many will have their morale affected by illness when you go into action in October. It's a lot cruder, but it can be done."

"Colds are one thing. What about courage?" The word came out sounding funny. It was not something Melton liked to talk about.

"Courage," Track said, "is a combination of how many colds a man has had and how many dear John letters and how drunk he was six weeks ago and how he feels from day to day about God, mother and the flag."

Melton stared. "That's all?"

"That's all the computer needs to know."

"Sir—"

"It can be done."

"Has it been?"

"Not in quite the way I have in mind," Track said. "But you'll see it work at the end of this sem—this cycle." He had almost said "semester."

Melton did not reply. He knew enough of war to disprize an easy psalm to courage, but enough of courage to feel contempt at the idea that it could be broken down into elements of casual joy and sorrow whose combination would not be equal to itself. He was willing to learn from Track how the wars of the future might be waged, but he was reluctant to hear a casual callow assessment

53

of how those of the past had been won, and he was not eager for the conversation to continue along this line. He had no wish to be rude to the officer.

But Track was looking at him expectantly.

In the orderly room, the electric clicking slackened from a chatter to a slap and then fell silent. The lieutenant looked at his watch. "Tell Reynolds he can take off. And then hang around for a minute if you would, first."

"Yes, sir."

When the orderly room was empty, Track lounged by Melton's desk, and the first sergeant waited silently to see what more he wanted. But the officer was pensive and remote. Perhaps he wanted nothing. Perhaps he wanted Melton's company. Melton wanted a drink.

"Is that a live round?" Track asked abruptly, indicating a bullet that sat on end on Melton's desk, carefully framed in the middle of a blank disposition form.

"It's live but it's harmless," Melton said, "more or less. It's like a blank. A new goody from our mad scientists." A slight hesitation marked his decision not to add: Something to improve the realism and effectiveness of the training.

Track picked it up. In appearance it was almost indistinguishable from a conventional round; perhaps it was a little lighter.

"A blank?"

He remembered his own training. The blanks he had used had looked like spent cartridges, crimped into a minuscule brass flower at the tip where the bullet ought to be, and they had not been harmless. The NCOIC had cautioned the men about that, advised them to fire into the air in the course of the exercise, not, in any case, into each other's faces, or at a range of less than fifty feet or so. *But they're just blanks.* The NCOIC had shrugged, fed a clip into his rifle, and fired two blanks at a heavy cardboard box, the muzzle far from touching, cocking the piece each time, for a

54

blank, unlike a bullet, will not eject automatically. The cardboard sprouted two jagged furry holes.

"Used like a blank in exercises. But that pellet at the front fires off like a bullet and marks whatever it hits. Naturally it hasn't got much range, and the trajectory is altogether different."

"Is it wax, or what?"

"Some kind of soft plastic compound, I think, sir. We've got a lot of paper work on it somewhere."

"What if it hits you in the face?"

"You ain't suppose to shoot anybody in the face with it, sir, or up close," Melton said. "But it'll make umpiring field problems and such a lot more exact," he added. "Ordnance has got it in stock now."

Track looked at the new false bullet. "Well, I'll be goddamned," he said slowly.

"We can draw 'em for your problem if you want, sir."

"Well, that may be up to the brain," Track said. It took Melton a moment to realize what he meant.

"I hope you don't leave too much up to that brain, lieutenant."

Track smiled. "I guess I'm one of the mad scientists, first sergeant?"

"I didn't say that, sir."

"See you in the morning, first."

"Lieutenant Track, if a man behaves well in combat, do you think it's enough to say he did so because he had hot food and a hard dick two days before, and a girl on the dock at home?"

Track sighed. "Let's bullshit about it later, all right?"

"Any time, sir."

When the lieutenant had left, as he did each afternoon promptly at the end of the duty day—after first locking the terminal, locking over it the hood he had had built for it, locking his desk, locking his office door—the first sergeant sat for a while in the orderly room, looking at a small book the officer had given him,

Track's monograph. *Inasmuch as a computer is a collection of circuits capable of existing in two states . . .*

After half an hour, he put on his gray plastic raincoat and his cap and went to the NCO Club. In its welcoming dark recess, he found a table, ignoring an invitation from the field first, who was drinking with two of the platoon sergeants at the bar. Melton drank whiskey sours slowly for an hour. He did not think about Track, or about computers, or about why men are sometimes very brave.

FOUR

FOUR

PENDLETON LURKED in the concrete pit, waiting for the voice from the tower. His dented helmet hung rakishly over his right eye, throwing stern shadows into his blank white face. On the sandbag beside him, his rifle lay with its muzzle pointed obediently downrange at the dark-green cardboard heads and shoulders scattered through the underbrush at intervals of fifty to three hundred meters. *Fifty meters*, the tower had said, *two hundred fifty meters. All targets up. All targets down.* Electronic hums filtered back to the men in the pits as the green paper forms lifted and fell.

Beside the rifle lay massive dominoes: clips. Spent shells swarmed restlessly over the cold ground.

Coaches, the tower said, *coach your firers into a good firing position. Firers, lock and load one six-round magazine. Ready on the right. Ready on the left. Ready on the firing line.*

"Can you manage all that?" Young asked politely. Pendleton hefted the rifle with more éclat than care, jammed in a random clip.

"I'll shit'n'sure try to be equal to the task." He brought his cheek down to the black plastic unreal form of the weapon, all knobs and points and angles. He pressed his cheek hard into the stock and got a good sight picture on nothing.

Commence firing, the tower said.

Pendleton saw a foe rise into the middle distance and put a round beneath it, launching a V of dust. "Low right," Young remarked indifferently. Pendleton fired again before the target could fall back, triumphant, fired overquick, but fortune blessed the bullet and the cardboard died.

"Ha," he said, "go and hang thyself, brave Young, for we have fought today at wherever, and you were not there."

"If you're gonna quote things at me, quote right. There's one at three hundred if you want it."

"I want it if I can see it." He could not. A target rose at fifty meters, shockingly close, and Pendleton felt an odd stab of fear: his imagination working on the Army's behalf. He shredded the left side of the target's head. . . .

Pendleton had come into the Army one rainy night at 2 A.M., stepping in weary confusion off a Trailways bus into a shapeless crowd of milling civilians who stood in a pool of light under the contemptuous gaze of a master sergeant and a coven of Sp4s. Somehow they were bent into a square in the rain and light and darkness. They were told to open their bags and spread the contents before them.

There is certain shit you can't have, and this is your one and only chance to get rid of it with no questions asked, the sergeant said. *Knives with more than a three-inch blade and any other weapons. Liquor, playing cards and any kind of drugs. Any pornography. You know what I mean, men, I mean those dirty books you have and you look at them and they're dirty.* He moved through the square, stopping occasionally, stopping in front of Pendleton.

What's in all those glasses cases, shitwick?

Glasses cases, sergeant.

You got glasses cases in those glasses cases?

60

G-glasses, sergeant.

No dirty pictures, son, nothing to look at and give that old whang a yank or two when you have a little free time, not that you will?

No, sergeant.

Pack it up.

The man next to Pendleton was a slender Negro wearing a letter jacket and a pair of deep-yellow wraparound dark glasses.

Get those shades off.

No.

No what?

No, sergeant.

Take them off.

No.

I'm not going to argue with you, son. He signaled. Two soldiers wearing MP brassards appeared behind the Negro and led him to the rear of the formation. Heads turned instinctively.

Don't look back there, the sergeant said, in a conversational tone that everybody could somehow hear. *You don't want to see what's going on back there.* He strode back to the front of the formation.

Sweet jumping Jesus, Pendleton thought—and it was for the first time, though several hours had elapsed since he raised his right hand—it's the Army, and I'm *in* it.

Men, the sergeant said, *welcome to the United States Army. Any questions? Never mind, I don't want to hear them.* Suddenly he roared, *Anybody want to go home?* Silence. *Nobody?* Silence. *Good. You* are *home. . . .*

The tower said:

Cease firing. Clear your weapons.

"You could have gone RA," Young said, as though picking up a thread of conversation. "You could have gone for one more lousy year, and right now you'd be learning how to file the morning report or how to fix a refrigerator or how to drive a truck, and instead you're still in the killing business."

"I'm not worried," Pendleton said, pulling himself out of the pit. "They put 'NCD' on my medical records."

"So?"

"That means 'No Combat Duty.'"

Young snickered. "Dreamer. It means 'Not Considered Disqualifying.'"

Pendleton stared at him.

A corporal, hard-stripe E-4—rare creature—stalked the path behind them. "Police up the brass, dickheads." He went on.

They began gathering up the shells. You would not have mistaken them for children in a meadow picking flowers. But Pendleton liked finding the shiny bits of yellow metal, hidden under rocks and sandbags, where they had been propelled by the rifle ejectors.

"How did you end up here anyway," Young demanded, "a bright guy like you?"

"I have friends in high places."

"Yeah, you gotta pull strings to wind up an Eleven Bravo, that's for certain."

"You know," Pendleton said, "I sort of like picking up brass. It's like finding Easter eggs."

"Oh, wow. Is policing up cigarette butts like pulling daisies? Or your pork?"

"You're soulless, Young. Soulless."

"I'm serious, though. How *did* you get here?"

"How did you?"

"Local board number whatever."

"Shake, friend."

"You could be wearing bars."

"I *could* be wearing civvies. But I ain't. Anyway, haven't we been through this movie before?"

62

"I just wondered."

Pendleton sighed. "You see before you a private soldier with a bachelor's degree in the history of science. Bang, bang."

"Drafted with the ink still wet on the diploma."

"Drafted before they even finished filling the fucker out."

"You could have headed for our neighbor to the north," Young suggested.

"You know . . . this may sound weird, but I never got as far as thinking about that. I'm damn sure not against it; I say God bless every dragging ass that made it to the border. But . . . I mean, I hate the fucking war and I have no intention of shooting anybody. But I hadn't thought about the Army very much. I thought I was going to grad school. When the greetings came, I went to basic instead. It was sort of automatic."

"Yeah," Young said, "things like that are sort of automatic. Being here is sort of accidental and automatic at the same time. And pretty soon we'll just get automatically sent where the fun is. And then maybe we'll just automatically kill somebody."

Pendleton straightened up, his cupped palms offering a spiky shiny gold bundle of shells. "Where do we go next?"

"We go eat out of mess kits and watch the National Guard company down the road eat out of trays."

"I like the Army," Pendleton said, "I really like it."

"You twenty-year men."

"Yeah. Two in and eighteen out."

They found their places in the files leaving the firing line and heading for the field kitchen, whose immersion-heater pipes could be seen behind the canvas tops of the trucks that sat high on the shoulder of the road. Rifles slung, they passed Cox, who was waiting by the range shack to hear the brief litany: "No brass, no ammo, sergeant . . . No brass, no ammo, sergeant." Two hours later, on the close-combat course, Cox saved Pendleton's life.

Probably . . .

The platoon sat in the warming hut, peacefully dazed by the heated darkness, few of them fighting off the central desire of the soldier, which is for sleep. Burning curls of tar paper and splinters of wood ripped from ammunition boxes cast an orange light through the open gate of the potbellied stove. The conversation of the drowsing men bore the muted stamp of midday speech when the speakers have been up since long before dawn and slept but briefly before.

". . . he said, 'You just salute field grade and above, soldier, or is this your day off, or what?' and I said, 'Why don't you take it in the left ear, lieutenant?' "

". . . yeah, that's right, that's what you said, all right."

". . . Germany. I'm going to Germany. I don't know about the rest of you sorry U.S. draftee bastards, but I got to choose where I was going when I signed up, and that's where."

". . . I'd eat a yard of her shit just to see where it came from."

". . . yeah, and you know what they do? They send you to Germany, all right, just like they promised. Then they bring your ass back one month later and stick it in the jungle for twelve months more."

The officer in charge of the course had finished his lecture, had left with his Masonite chart board and its handsome plastic overlays. The NCOs who worked with him had gone out to walk over the ground one more time before they turned the trainees loose on it. This was a potentially very dangerous exercise, perhaps even more so than the infiltration course, because the men would be moving around, getting ahead of each other and trailing behind, firing live ammunition at targets which would pop toward them from many shapes and shades and forms of cover. But as the platoon waited to be called to its hazardous chore, it largely slept.

"Can you keep all that shit straight in your mind, Mr. Pendleton?" Young mumbled. He was sitting with his weapon across his pressed knees, back sharply erect, pretending he was an airborne Ranger waiting for the green light. "Airborne" had been a PT cry from the first day of basic, though it was unlikely that many of these draftees had an unquenchable desire to jump from a moving airplane. Young thought of Sergeant Alestock, the forty-five-year-old black paratroop staff sergeant who had literally run in circles around the jogging, shuffling column of weak young men, his hard wise smile, his continual proud taunt:

"Whiskey!"

—*Whiskey!*

"No good!"

—*No good!*

"Women!"

—*Women!*

"No good!"

—*No good!*

"PT!"

—*PT!*

"So good!"

—*So good!*

Young's question canceled Pendleton's familiar reverie: was there a world outside, a world which prepared breakfast and read stock market reports and dressed fish, or had he been here forever —always weary, always running, always oiling leather and polishing metal—and only dreamed the other?

"My mind's OK," Pendleton told him. "I can't say I'm overjoyed at the idea of you behind me, squeezing off live stuff."

"Trust me, I'm a killer."

"I believe it. But I'm too young."

"No, I'm too young."

Small wit. Well, they were tired, and the Army had shown them again and again what small use it had for verbal cleverness. It was

65

a fine discipline for the mind in its own strange way, Pendleton thought, the Army: monastery of harm, where clarity and brevity are loved, and choked with jargon.

They sank back into lethargy, rousing occasionally to throw a butt into the stove, to sip metal water from their canteens. Perhaps they thought about the live ammunition in their weapons.

"You ever pull guard?" Young asked after a while.

"Sure. Once. In basic."

"They paint the tips of the bullets?"

"Yes." *If you do fire a round, your poor old platoon sergeant will need to fill out a stack of paper work this thick to explain how come you did it. So don't fire a round.*

"Ever challenge anybody?"

"Just the relief."

"Didn't you feel like shooting off those bullets just because you had them? At a tree or something?"

"No," Pendleton said.

"You know Sergeant Cox killed a guy once? Sort of."

Pendleton looked at him. "You mean that guy that went AWOL in the cycle before us? He just caught him. Some MP killed him. It was an accident."

"Sure," Young muttered. "Yeah, it's always an accident."

"What makes you bring that up?"

"This." Young patted his rifle. "I wonder what it feels like."

"It would probably give you an erection."

"It would probably make Cox shoot his load."

"Why don't you ease up?" Pendleton demanded. "What's he done to you in the last ten minutes?"

"You know he's got a wife?" another soldier said. With his interruption, the conversation in the hut gave promise of becoming general. "Cox."

"Seems I heard that."

"He never mentions her."

"What do you expect?" Pendleton countered. "You usually get a lot of conversation from NCOs on their private lives?"

"I had a detail cleaning his room," the soldier said. "He doesn't even have a picture of her on his table."

"At least he's got a table."

"He prob'ly makes her lie at attention."

"Nah, parade rest."

"Christ," said Pendleton. "You fucking guys. One thought. One topic. One way of expressing it."

"Cunt—ten*hut!* Col'm lieft—*come!*"

There was some laughter.

Sergeant Cox threw open the hut door. "All right, fourth platoon, let's go. Outside—move."

Sunlight stabbed through the fountains of pine needles, lay in geometrical ponds on the pattern of logs and boulders, foxholes and tree trunks, that stretched away from their feet as they stood at the start of the course.

"Fourth platoon, fall in," Cox said softly. "Dress it tight and get your intervals." *Dress right dress and cover down, forty inches all around* . . . "Tay*hut.* At ease. Odd men are A. Even are B. Sound off with it."

Pendleton was momentarily confused. He tried to remember what the course OIC had said.

" 'toon, tay*hut.* Forrard, *harch.* 'toon, *hawt.* At ease. Get into your teams and get to the starting point. Lock and load."

"Column a twos from the right—"

"Forward—"

"—stand fast!"

"—*harch!*"

Cox was giving his commands indifferently today, as though they were laundry lists.

Pendleton and Young, A and B, took up their positions. Pendleton squinted down the fire lane that lay before him, finding his first cover, locating the probable point of rise of his first target. Behind him and Young stood Sergeant Cox, the rim of his blue helmet liner resting on the bridge of his nose, eyes at a slow hard dance in the black well of the helmet's shadow, head tilted back and hips thrust forward, thumbs in his pistol belt, the classic pose of a small-town small-time street-corner hood, and a dated one at that. Pendleton, snapping a clip into his rifle, glancing back at Cox, seemed to see the outline of a pompadoured petty thief in pink shirt and charcoal slacks lost in the hard clean motionless body of the young sergeant.

The rattle of a whistle cracked the bell of fall air.

"A man, move out!" Young shouted, finding a layer of thunder for his voice, an offering for the sergeant.

"B man, cover me!"

Pendleton, as he yelled, was running forward in a crouch, bent over his rifle, throwing himself behind a log, knees down with a fast painful crash, leaning into the butt of the weapon, now the rifle raised in supplication to keep it above the cold rising dust, as Young, prone behind him, fired two rounds left into the target zone ahead. Pendleton thought he could hear the passing of the bullets. Chamber pressure 50,000 pounds per square inch. No, that was the M-14. No . . . There were tiny tears, cones of yellow dirt from the target zone. He caught his breath, found a sight picture. "Move out!" Young came stumbling past him, standing too high, his rifle held before him at hip level.

"Cover me!"

"Move out!"

"Cover me!"

They worked the lane that way, increasingly slowly, Cox walking behind, as ragged high reports of gunfire sounded from the lanes on either side. Cox walked erect, alert, just behind the slow weaving line of mock conflict, his heart working faster as a blanket of cordite fumes rose from the weapons. His glittering boots, their heels and soles enameled to a black as resonant as the polished patent leather of their surfaces, ground rings of falling fallen brass into the dirt. The cries from the moving men began to take tone, intensity, ferocity as they wandered heavily through the dry mist of battle.

Cox watched his two men with some satisfaction. Pendleton, pussy though he was, was reading his movements right out of the book, body bent and weapon protected, low-crawling swiftly, firing carefully and often accurately. Young was less exact, he would die early in combat, but he was full of energy and eagerness to please. The two had left behind them an adequate trail of cardboard dead.

Now the squad was closing in on its objective. The line was surprisingly even, the firing steady. Dust from the earth and burning powder from the M-16s mingled in a proud gift for the sergeant's nostrils. His hands began to sweat.

At the end of the course was a small lake. High rounds were already tearing climbing white stalagmites of water out of its blue winking surface. On the shore of the lake, at the end of the lanes, the final objective stood, a squad of silent still packed canvas cylinders strung into wooden frames, calmly waiting the attack. The squad would kill its last paper targets, the B men would sprawl behind their final cover, the A men would fix bayonets and charge the dummies, walking, shouting, firing from the hip their remaining rounds, then close with steel for the kill, bayoneting, butt-stroking, slashing, stabbing, screaming, striking, choking, destroying. The mission of the infantry is to close with the enemy and destroy him. Queen of battles. O God of battles . . .

The A man would move carefully back, enemy vanquished, duty done. The B man would mimic him.

"Move out!"

"Cover me!"

Cox watched his men close in. He was almost ready, in the

69

moment, to call them soldiers. The dummy on the shore swam in his vision as he broke into a slight run behind them. With desperate joy, he willed them to be gone, their weapons in his own empty hands, the canvas shape before him to be living flesh, a breathing adversary to seek his death, a man for him to close with, that they might dispute four feet of ground, and die. . . .

"Move out!"

Cox paused at last behind Young as the trainee sprawled into a gully, sweating and sandy, rifle jammed. Young cursed. The sergeant pulled the weapon away and cleared it, crouched by Young, still holding it, watching as Pendleton began his walk.

"Kill him!" Cox heard his voice come hoarsely. "*Kill him!*"

The private had begun at a shy stumble, reticent at the heavy melodrama of his chore. He jumped, as though physically jolted. In the spell of an instinct beyond volition, he had recognized in Cox's command the order to which all the Army's other orders stand as servant. He might yet despise the understanding, but now, at last, he would obey the instinct. Let it be a lie, a game, or a moral disaster, it was *real*. And Pendleton, who had spent much of his life discarding things he loved as they lost reality for him, responded to it. He started shouting, emptying his rifle from the hip with a spray of full automatic, smashing sand and lifting water, tearing gray clouds from his target and showers of raw red wood from its frame. Along the line, firing sputtered, staggered, and stopped; rifles fell silent, Pendleton's with them. The shouting continued. He went into a jerky run, roaring the requisite anger, closing the distance. Pendleton, who, at his own immodest evaluation, had spent twenty years learning to value human life, took the dummy's with bullet and steel. He stabbed, slashed, tore, butt-stroked. Cox watched in wonderment. It was too fine to be an act. And yet it was too much to hope that Pendleton had finally found his enemy. But sufficient unto the day. Pendleton was killing. That was how Sergeant Cox saved his life.

FIVE

THE POST

was 'huge. It spread over thousands of acres in the northeast corner of the state, dotting its tiny white-stenciled matériel over broad green weedy fields choked with fingers of forest, over endless and sourceless narrow trails bent under rivers of sand. There was a small lake, a smaller river —a stream, really—and an extensive area cloaked in walls of green and wells of wet that, very nearly, was a swamp.

Beside the post, on flatter fields, lay an Air Force base. Sometimes, when a company was moving from the dark shape of its barracks onto one of the narrow sandy paths that led into the destined forest of its march, the sand a tiny trail of pearl in the dim light of 4 A.M., with the moon still strong and the mists of dawn a dawn away from rising—sometimes that company would be going into the sand, sapped and quiet at the prospect of a long march and a longer day, but still noisy with the massive muted unending noise of a moving column, the small continuing rattle of sock-wrapped forks in metal mess kits, the shifting of packs to get them as high on the back as they would possibly go, the myriad damp canvas snaps of rifle slings being adjusted, canteens bobbing on a wave of olive thighs, dog tags swinging free of wet laboring chests and meeting at the end of their chains with a tiny sound,

73

scabbards slapping, and the slow ordered crush into the sand of four hundred boots—sometimes, then, that company beginning its day's work would follow, double file, a path that led it along the fence that separated the post from the Air Force base; and, out of the flat dark beyond, the men would see the colored lights of the runways and the tall, light-guttering candle of the tower, and the low, largely unlit building around it, dumb profile showing darker blue on blue. And then a sound would commence far off, and grow, and a shape grow with it, and the men would flinch under the growing keening explosive growling roar as it swept past fifty feet above them, the tumultuous mass of a jet fighter, pulling its afterburners with it like an afterthought, two soft orange bowls of fire in the dark. Then the sound would die, silence would replace it, and the silence would be filled again by the small long noise of the company.

Track took his company into such a dark march one day that fall. Their destination was a bivouac area near the spot where, near the end of the cycle, Track's company would engage an Aggressor force in a mirror of combat. The lieutenant was eager to see the place. Until now, he had known it only from maps and charts, and it was necessary that he know it firsthand, and well, for an exact description of the area, rendered into terms his computer could relish, would furnish parameters in his search for optimum conditions for the deployment of his men when it came time to send them into battle, into a simulacrum of battle.

First Sergeant Melton had, days before, with the ruthless logic of a mind unpolluted by the excitement of technology, raised an objection. "Lieutenant, if you need to know the location of every blade of grass on the ground you're gonna be fighting on before you can get your electric brain squared away, what the hell use is it?"

Track had pointed out the staggering mass of information available to computer matrices pondering global war.

"Sure—sir—because just like you said, in that case the information is usable in a more general form. But the situation you're anticipating will require that you have instantaneous and fluid knowledge—no, I mean complete static knowledge of a fluid situation. And a squad assaulting an outhouse ain't gonna have time to radio back the color of the toilet paper so you can ask the brain whether they should throw a grenade, fix bayonets or haul ass."

"Stop calling it a brain," Track said irritably.

Melton was fundamentally correct. The commander could have entwined his first sergeant in a dialogue on the question that might ultimately have forced Melton into supplying the wrong reasons for the right judgment, but that would be a pallid triumph. The fact remained, and Track brooded on it as he marched silently beside Sergeant First Class Sherman, who was setting the pace at the head of the column. Army brass—not just those on post, but more than one man in the Pentagon itself—would be watching his experiment with skeptical interest. Here, after all, was what amounted to the final confrontation of the ultimate weapon, the foot soldier, with the new power that guided his feet.

Put so baldly, Track disliked the idea, disliked the cultural melodrama inherent in it. His plan was at once revolutionary and modest. It did not conceive of each infantryman as a readout from a metal mind, despite what, say, Major Haslip might think. It was simply a question of the fresh application of concepts, nothing more than the logical extension—

Correct—no, probably worse than just correct. The question was not only one of a satisfactorily complete prior knowledge of terrain, which was never going to be as plausible in combat as in training; it also awoke a new awareness of the infinitely multiplied difficulties of maintaining complete communication with an element in contact with the enemy. It was one thing for a radioman to call in for artillery, air support, reinforcements, ammuni-

75

tion, medics, a dustoff; quite another to expect him to be able to feed back the kind of exhaustive data the matrix would hunger for—let alone translate it on the spot into a usable tongue. Well, there was the middleman for that. But still: the information failure, the time delay.

No, Track thought, dammit, no. Repairable. All repairable. He accepted the fact that his concept might work at first in garrison and kill fifty men in the field; that was all right; it would end in increased efficiency, in tighter, faster, more flexible control by corps and division of company and squad. He could—he would— work out the bugs. A thin line of pure thought would run like an antenna from the point of every bayonet to the center of some unflawed brain. Every pfc a PhD! Lovely. He'd see and be the be he saw—

"Givem ten, sir?" Sherman murmured. Track looked at his watch. They were well into the trees now, and though the sky above the fields had begun to turn a colorless pink, erasing the stars and fading the quarter moon, here they were in darkness, and the circle of radium dots strapped to his wrist blurred slightly as the lieutenant lifted his arm toward his face. They had left the company area just under an hour ago.

"Givem five, sergeant."

Track leaned against a tree and took one of his long cigarettes out of the pocket of his fatigue shirt, where it had lain loose, bent and partly crumpled. He lighted it.

"Take five!"

"—five!"

He had let Ballanger set too sharp a pace and let his own pride bluff him into too short a break; his chest knew heavy motion, the skin above his collarbone was dewed with fine sweat. And, to his surprise, his genitals were telegraphing a noticeable hunger. He adjusted the crotch of his fatigue pants, letting his fingers dig briefly into the swelling. Here, for Christ's sake, and now. He had

76

been up late the night before preparing for this march, and exhaustion had washed his sleep of dreams. So why? He took his hand away.

He looked down the column. As far as he could see, men were folding and slipping into the dark sides of the path with motions as grateful as the glide of an undersize trout from an angler's hand into cool water.

"—five!"

The call was going down the column. The noise increased. Still there were no voices save those of the NCOs.

"Smokem if you gottem."

"You!" Sherman's ears seemed to have chosen from the feast of minor sound the uncurling plastic noise of a canteen cap being unscrewed. "If I see you take a slug of that water, trooper, you'll pour the rest of it on the ground. We aren't hardly started. You don't need that water yet."

Track, his mouth dry and sour in the first rush of cigarette smoke, had been about to reach for his own canteen. He sighed and stood up. There was surely some duty he was called to while his men rested, but he could not think what it might be.

The company was in bivouac by late afternoon. Track, subtly assisted by Sherman and Melton, had seen to the conjunction of shelter halves, the digging of latrines, the hanging of lister bags, the posting of guards, the full tangle of detail that presented its unvarying bill whenever two hundred men must make a single sweep of earth their home for one day, one night, no more.

The lieutenant stood by his tent, watching the platoons form chow lines. He had managed to consume several candy bars—unnoticed, he believed—during the march, and he was not hungry. He felt a curious contentment. A little heat had come into the day, and a narrow breeze was toying with the concave canvas walls of the command-post tent. His equipment lay on a table inside;

after the weary dull agony of the march, when every strap and buckle had seemed finally to be hooked to the earth he moved on like metal strands of quicksand dragging him down futher with each step, the sole weight of the pistol belt seemed to be a girl's hands on his waist.

Melton came up to the tent and saluted him. "Sir, will you want a recon patrol?"

Track returned the salute slowly, to mask his surprise. It had not occurred to him. This was a bivouac, fun in the field, no more. There were no Aggressor troops. But he said:

"Yeah, I guess so. Have—have Sergeant Cox send some of his people out."

Melton did not miss the uncertainty. "It's just SOP, sir."

"Yeah, I know," said Track. Some of his pleasure in the day was gone. He dismissed the first sergeant and went into the tent. Thirty minutes later, the patrol radioed in.

Track was sitting at a field table cleaning his pistol when the radio sputtered on and an excited voice swam through the static. "—hear me. Over."

The CP radioman was an unkempt-looking pfc who had been reading a fat yellow paperback. He reached for his mike slowly and pushed the button in.

"Tiger two, this is tiger one, I hear you five by. Over."

"Tiger one, this is tiger two. We have contact with Outlaw. Over."

"Authenticate," Track snapped. His radioman fumbled briefly with the SOI manual.

"Tiger two, this is tiger one. Authenticate niner Alpha. Over."

There was a short pause, and then the whisper returned through the static. "Tiger one, I authenticate niner Alpha as Tango Tango. Over."

"They're real, sir," the pfc said.

"Right. Get the dope."

"Tiger two, this is tiger one. Repeat—"

"*Damn* it," Track said. He put his pistol down. "What the hell do you mean, 'Repeat'?"

"I'm sorry, sir."

"Sorry don't work, sorry don't save lives. You're a-fucking-well-number-one-told you'd be sorry if an artillery outfit picked up your sending and dropped a fire mission on your ass."

"Yes, sir."

"Let me have the phone. Tiger two, this is tiger six. What the hell is going on? Say again all after—no, say again all message. Over."

"Tiger one, this is tiger two. I say again we have Outlaw contact. Over."

"Never mind the trimmings. What's up? Over."

It was critically wrong. Track had taken the radioman up short for saying "repeat" for "say again"; and now in the next breath he was dispensing with proper radio procedure.

"Sir, we have contact with Outlaw in platoon strength headed for the perimeter. Over."

"Who is this? Over."

"Sir, Private Pendleton. Over."

Track tried to get his thoughts together. There wasn't supposed to *be* any Aggressor force out there on this fine autumn afternoon. He had no idea of the composition of his own patrol, or of its exact assigned mission. "Tiger two, this is tiger one. Break contact and return to base. Over."

"Sir," Pendleton said, "I don't think we can."

Pendleton had been sitting in front of his shelter half pretending to be cleaning verdigris from his bayonet when Sergeant Cox called his name. He struggled to his feet, the blade still in his hand, squinting into the caramel arms of sunlight that came in bars through the overcast.

79

"Yes, sergeant?"

Cox came up to him. The dust of the march had climbed to the knees of the sergeant's fatigues, but there was no other sign that he had been moving hard since before daybreak. Pendleton was himself still more than a little tired. He found it hard to believe the march was really over, and that he had finished it on his feet: several of the company had not. When last he had heard Cox's voice, it had been raised in a cracked shout—*Porwt—hahms! Doubletime—harch*—and Pendleton had, for the tenth time that day, swung the weight of his rifle off his shoulder and let it fall into his open hand, lifted his feet from the sucking sand into an agonized rapid shuffle, into the impossibly demanded, impossibly performed, run. But the march was over, the bivouac made. It was time to find some tiny chore, to feign a duty and capture a rest. But when Cox stopped in front of him, Pendleton, as usual, caught himself tensing as though he were about to come to attention.

"Yes, sergeant?" he said again.

"Pendleton, come with me."

"Where to, sergeant?"

"Little walk. You'll love it if you think about it the right way. Bring your gear."

"What's the story?"

"You're the story. I'm letting you play honcho. You're gonna take a squad out and wander around the boonies for a while. Recon. Do a decent job and I'll think about putting a rocker on your stripe one of these days."

Pendleton realized the sergeant meant it, and felt a small point of pleasure catching hold within him. That bothered him. He was always a little sorry when some aspect of the Army made him respond to it as a professional might.

"Take a radioman and six others," Cox said. "Take your buddy Young. Carry a knife in your teeth and a tommy gun in each hand." *You think this exercise is funny, young man? You think this exercise is a joke?*

"Yes, sergeant."

"Go about a thousand meters into the trees across from the north perimeter and take a look around. Work back to the west."

"What do we look for, sergeant?"

"The enemy."

"But there isn't any."

"There's always an enemy," Cox said. "Move out."

Pendleton, with no small embarrassment, explained his new command position to Young, who gave him a mocking salute and a loud curse. "It's not enough we walk our asses off all morning. It's not enough we have to take turns walking in fucking circles around this place all night. Now we have to wander in the wilderness all afternoon looking for the bad guys. Come on, man. I vas on ze Rooshian front, I nefer saw an Amerikan soldier. Get somebody else."

"Cox said take you," Pendleton insisted.

"I say take gas." But Young struggled, cursing, back into his pack and picked up his rifle. "What makes him so fucking interested in you, anyway?"

"He mistakes me for a soldier," Pendleton said. "It's not his fault; the light's dim."

"He's an asshole."

"He's good at his job," Pendleton said flatly.

"So was Hitler."

"Young," said Pendleton slowly, "don't settle for wisecracks and easy answers. Sergeant Cox isn't a monster."

"You've been doing deep thinking again. Didn't I warn you about that?"

"No—simple pragmatism. There is a point where certain kinds of well-bred revulsions lose their practical value. I think maybe we missed it, somewhere back when they first gave us weapons

81

and tried to teach us to use them." He looked away. "I don't like Cox or what he stands for. But every once in a while I do remember that what he's teaching me might save my ass. All the ethical shit does is save my soul. You put your soul and your ass in the balance sometime, buddy, and take a hard look. And tell me which is heavier."

"All right, Beau Geste," Young said sourly. "Pick up the rest of your shock troops and let's get the fucking show on the sucking road."

"That's the s-fucking-how on the r-sucking-oad."

"Beautiful."

They moved single file out of the bivouac area, Pendleton at the point. They had smeared their faces with green and black grease and had tangled weeds and vines in the cloth covers of their helmets. They were playing the game. His eight men were very silent; too often, Pendleton turned back to look at them. They came toward him as though they were marching to the tap of a drum.

At the tree line, Pendleton halted, and his men bunched up. Young took out a pack of cigarettes.

"Who called a smoke break?"

"What?"

"Who called a smoke break?" Pendleton said.

Young looked at him. Then he put the pack back into his pocket. Young kept his cigarette pack inside a metal case and the case inside a rubber. People who laughed at the elaborateness in garrison bummed smokes from him in the field.

The woods were thick, but there was little underbrush. The floor of the forest was like a floor. Through the triple canopy of the trees, sun fell in darkness like shifting yellow trunks. Pendleton was not entirely sure how he should deploy his men as they went into the trees, but he knew they should not be bunched together. "Keep your distances," he said. He started off ahead of them, unslinging his rifle and bringing it to the port.

He let himself pretend he was a soldier, let himself hear the drum. There was no point in not doing it; it made the senseless job bearable, almost entertaining. As a child, he had played with toy soldiers; no doubt all boys do. But his games had been lengthy and complex, they had covered rooms and embraced armies, leaden and plastic, tiny bits of soldiers in the shape of Caesar and Custer and the twentieth century indiscriminately mixing their quarrel, swarming on furniture, down creek beds of rugs, into forts of cardboard and old castles of wood. Very well. He would be a soldier now and play with—

The ground in front of him sent up a section of itself with a sharp noise like the snapping of a wide dry root; the section separated into chunks and tufts lifted by a fan of dust. A soft wave hit him.

He froze.

To his left, he heard the tapping of an automatic weapon, remote in his clouded ear. There were other small noises. A wide low band of yellow smoke began to roll in from the right. He could see no one.

"Take cover," he said, in tones barely above the conversational, feeling stupid. The men, in one clumsy way or another, had already done so. As he slumped in weary confusion behind a tree, Pendleton saw Young fall into a hollow to his left, the radioman behind him, the antenna of his walkie-talkie whipping through a lazy arc.

The smoke moved closer, and Pendleton managed a shout:

"Mask and fire into the smoke! Somebody spot that machine gun!" Plastic bullets began splattering around him. He reached down his right hip, unsnapping the gas mask container, and dragged the ugly black rubber snout up his side. It got dirty. He

83

knocked off his helmet and jammed his chin into the cup of the mask. "Radio the CP—tell them we've got a contact—get instructions—" He had the mask tightened as the smoke swept over them. He still saw no one in the trees beyond. He fired a blank. The machine gun tapped again on his left. Firing came from the right. Some of his own men had begun to fire now. . . .

Himself, he thought, with himself, as in the wars of lead and plastic that ended with no man alive: toy after toy scattered on the wool/rayon/nylon/dacron battlefield in twisted manners weighted with disaster: heads and arms severed by a razor, streaks of red dope disfiguring die-cast faces and dripping, drooling, down bent multicolored legs; the forts of cardboard charred by real flame, bodies of men melted by the same searching fire—there was even smoke and dust and weird winking waves of shadow and light. There was even a special silence. Three feet higher, magazines might litter a coffee table. Here there had been a battle. He had toy soldiers, but he made them die real deaths. . . .

The radioman had raised the CP. Pendleton crawled to him and took the phone. There was confusion and foolishness at the other end, and a long waste of time by details of cipher. He spoke to the CO and was told to fall back. But the firing continued, and by now it seemed to be on all sides. Then the smoke thinned, and figures came out of it at last, jaunty in caps and camouflage, weapons slung and finally silent. Pendleton rested his rifle against a root, bolt up and open. On his left flank, some of his men continued firing their blanks, and he raised his hand for them to stop.

The ambushers were Disenhaus and Rellin—two of the platoon sergeants—and Cox. Cox stopped by Pendleton and picked up the phone. "It's just smoke," he said, before he pushed the button, and Pendleton took off his mask. So did Young and the radioman. The yellow smoke had thinned out along the ground now in a fine grainy mist.

"Tiger one, this is tiger two. How do you hear me? Over," Cox said. His face was smeared, dark.

"Tiger two, this is tiger one. I hear you five by. What the hell do you mean you can't break contact? Over."

"Tiger one, this is Outlaw," Cox said. "Tiger two can't break contact because they're all dead. Out."

The radio came back with something.

"No speak English," Cox said. "*Out.*" He gave the field phone back to the radioman. "All right, people, gather round. Smokem if you gottem."

Pendleton's men came over. They sat in a semicircle around the ambushers.

"Sergeant Disenhaus? Sergeant Rellin?" Cox said politely.

"No, go ahead, sergeant."

Cox was about to speak when the radio intruded again. "Turn that thing off, troop. The old man still thinks he can make radio contact with a bunch of guys who just got greased." He lighted a cigarette.

"Don't leave that weapon on the ground like that," Sergeant Rellin said quietly to one of the men.

"All right," Cox said, "here's the word. Like I said, you're all dead. Every one of you. That's for four reasons. One. You took forever finding cover. In the first place, you should have spotted us fifty meters back, we weren't all that well concealed. But even after that charge went off under your noses, you stood around and gaped for a good three seconds. That was all the time we needed."

"Sergeant—"

"Hold onto it. Two, you were all uptight together. One grenade would have taken out most of the patrol.

"Three. Once you did take cover, it was another five seconds before you started firing. More time on our side. *Time,* gentlemen.

85

"And four. Most of you waited to find a target. People, in an ambush in this kind of terrain, you aren't going to see anybody. So don't wait. Throw every bit of fire you can into the direction from which you're being fired on. *React.* Living through an ambush depends on your reaction time, and it depends on an aggressive response. Your chances aren't very good anyway, but that's the only chance at all. Sergeants?"

"Nothing," said Rellin.

"Make noise," Disenhaus offered. "You've been told that. Scream and yell. Also, you—Young—you gave some security to the radioman. That was good." It had been a coincidence.

"All right," Cox went on, "yeah, that was good. And you made some other good moves, mainly you, Pendleton, you dickhead—you looked a little bit like a soldier for a minute there. You gave commands, if it did take you the best part of an hour to do it and the best part of another to find some balls to back your voice with. You thought to mask when you saw the smoke—"

"Yes," said Rellin, "right, but you shouldn't all be masking at one time, right? Else who's covering? Right? Excuse me, sergeant."

"Right, thank you, sergeant. Yeah. But you *did* mask; and you made radio contact pretty quick; and you had your men fire into the smoke, which was correct, because smoke is always covering something, right?" He thought a minute. "You better learn to tell the difference between a light automatic rifle and a machine gun, troop."

"By sound?" Pendleton wondered.

"Well, they ain't gonna supply a blueprint, baby." Cox walked on his cigarette until it was under the black dirt. "So that's about it. You're dead, but you died doing it the right way. Next time, get yourselves together faster, and some of you will walk away just wounded. OK, Pendleton, fall your patrol in and movem back to the bivouac area."

When the young soldiers had gone, the three sergeants re-

86

mained in the little clearing. Cox sat down on a stump with a sharp tired exhalation and unscrewed his canteen cap. He juggled a mouthful of water on his tongue, spat it out, and swallowed another. The other two men sat on the ground. Rellin said:

"You talk about smoke covering something. Smoke is gonna cover your U.S. draftee ass when Mr. Track gets the story together."

"It wasn't exactly my idea," said Cox, "not that I give a shit. Those guys get into combat, there won't be rules that say this bivouac is safe and this one isn't. Nothin wrong with shakin' up the program a little." He regretted referring to combat that way. He had never been in combat and the other two men had. But they said nothing.

"Whose idea was it?" Disenhaus wanted to know.

"Well, mine as much as anybody's."

"Come on, Billy, don't talk shit to me."

"Melton's. Sergeant Melton's."

"First Sergeant Melton," said Rellin.

"He's not like that."

"No," Rellin agreed, "he's not. He's a damned good man. But I think he's worried about Mr. Track's fun and games."

"Maybe so," Cox said.

"Was this little stunt dreamed up to make the lieutenant think about it harder before he starts fucking over the troops with his handy-dandy mind-finder?"

"How would I know?"

"Because Melton thinks a lot of you," Disenhaus said, "though I'm damned if I know why. You're a sorry sergeant."

"You're a cunt," Cox said.

"I'm a dehydrated cunt."

Cox passed over his canteen. "They didn't do all that badly," he said, after a silent moment had passed.

"No. They didn't. They weren't all dead, either."

"Well, I didn't want anybody to feel left out."

"That kid you put in charge must have done some shaping up."

"Pendleton? Yeah. Some. He used to be a sad mother jumper. He's got about a dozen degrees."

"Say what?"

"College degrees. He went to college."

"Why ain't he an officer?"

"Why ain't you an officer?"

"Why ain't *you* an officer?"

"Why don't you both shut the fuck up," Rellin said. "You make all the money you got time to spend right the way you are."

"Speaking of which," Disenhaus offered, "all Lieutenant Track is going to do with his computer is add a few thousand dollars to the cost of killing a man. You know how much it used to cost to kill a man in Vietnam? One single solitary slope? I think the figure was ten thousand dollars, that's what it comes out to. Or a hundred thousand, I'm not right sure. Anyway, a lot. That's counting everything, of course."

"Wasn't that expensive for everybody." Rellin said. "I was with an outfit right next a Marine rifle company, they were mostly snipers. Weird guys. Had hunting rifles and old Springfields and all kinds of shit. They used to sit up in trees, hours at a time, quiet as leaves, with scopes, until they saw a good target, usually nothing less than a field-grade officer. They could hit him through five hundred meters of jungle. Poor bastard thought he was safe, and there'd be the angel of death in his mouth before he could holler." The staff sergeant rummaged through his shirt for a book of matches. "The rounds they used cost thirteen cents apiece. Thirteen cents to kill some big-shot slope. And they never used but one bullet per man."

"That's real cost-effective," Cox said. Suddenly he wanted to be alone. It came on him with the shock and swiftness of a blow. There were some things he wanted to say about the mock ambush they had just staged, something about the way he felt, but it could not be to these two men, probably not to anybody. So he wanted to be by himself. But he could think of no way to get off by himself. "They should have fixed bayonets," he said.

"What the fuck? Who?"

"These kids," Cox said impatiently. "Today."

"It doesn't really make that much difference," Rellin answered. "You don't get many chances to use one any more. Like hand-to-hand. They just study these things now kind of like studying history. It's like you said earlier. All you can mostly do is spray wherever they're spraying you from. And not many men, even good soldiers, like to use bayonets. It's a hard thing to do."

Cox took a chance. "You ever do it?"

"No. I had a shotgun. But I saw it done."

"Jesus," Disenhaus muttered, "a war story. Tell me a war story, Daddy."

This was not as good as being alone, but it seemed to help in somewhat the same way. Cox said, "Here, take one of mine."

"No, man, that's cancer. You're smoking cancer there. Um. I saw it done to a prisoner."

"Jesus."

"Yeah. We had two and we needed some information out of at least one of them in a bad way."

"That's not quite what I meant." Cox remembered a class he had had in basic on the handling of prisoners. *Sir, what if he makes a run for it?* The officer had grinned and pantomimed squeezing off a clip. *Twelve extra assholes.*

"I know it ain't."

"I don't think I could do that," Cox said.

"I don't suppose anybody could who wasn't sick," Rellin answered. "Fortunately, we had a man who was."

"Let's get moving," Disenhaus said, standing up. "Let's get on back."

89

. . . He had not been a twenty- or thirty-year man, but he had not been a draftee, either. He was on his second enlistment when he came as a replacement to the base camp out of which Rellin's company operated. Rellin was an Sp4 then, a squad leader, and the man had come into his squad. He was the fifth replacement they had needed in the last seven months.

He fit in well. He was quiet and efficient, visibly very frightened for a longer time than most of the men had been, but he did his job, and Rellin saw that he didn't keep to himself and brood too much.

Their company was then in a backwater. They had their patrols and their ambushes, their search-and-clear missions, but they were no longer doing heliborne assaults, and they were no longer taking casualties with the regularity they had been, or inflicting them, either.

Nevertheless, the new man was very cautious for a long time. But he did not flake out on them, or refuse to make the patrols and the missions and the ambushes. In fact, he often held up his end with a seasoned competence that wore oddly with his caution.

Most of the other men now traveled as lightly as they could, except that they carried a lot of extra ammunition, and the squad leaders and the platoon sergeants no longer got on them for it. But the new man always wore his flak jacket and his steel pot. He carried two extra bandoliers of ammunition for his rifle and a trench knife as well as a bayonet. Grenades swarmed on his chest like clumps of iron feces.

After he had been with them about a month, they sprang an ambush on a patrol of NVA regulars. The new man did well. He killed two men with a grenade and helped kill a third with a burst from his rifle, and wounded a fourth; Rellin killed that one himself.

It was the new man's first action, and Rellin made a point of complimenting him on the way he had handled himself. The man looked at him blankly and said, *But there wasn't anything in it. There wasn't anything going on. Nothing happened.* Rellin didn't say anything more to him after that. He realized later that by "nothing happened," the man had of course meant that nothing had happened to him.

After that, the new man wore only a brimmed canvas hat and no flak jacket, like the rest of them, and carried only what he needed to get by with.

They went on for another long period with no activity save for the endless infinite monotonous beating of the white sun and the scraping and sawing of the grass at their pants legs. Then one day they were ambushed in their turn, and this time the new man was hit, but not before he had killed one enemy soldier with his rifle and another with his bayonet. He was not badly hurt. He was back with them in two weeks. When he got back to the company, Rellin said to him jokingly, *I guess something happened that time, huh?*

The man said, *Yes, it was a little better.*

It was shortly after that that they took the two prisoners and needed the information without delay. The new man went to where the two prisoners were tied and bayoneted one. The other supplied the information.

Rellin told him, *You could be court-martialed for that. And I think I want to see you court-martialed for it. I'm sure I do.*

But nothing was ever done.

Later on in the year, the squad flushed a sniper. The VC fell into the underbrush, face glazed with red, wounded but still very much in business. The new man closed in on him and killed him with a knife.

You got a rifle, Rellin said. *It works, don't it? It has rounds in it, don't it? So why do it the hard way? You could have shot him without any danger to yourself or the rest of us.*

By that time, no one was talking to the new man socially. . . .

91

Rellin seemed inclined to let the story drift at that point. They were almost at the bivouac area. White smoke was sopping from the immersion heaters—that was the first thing visible—and the first sound audible was the faint tinny noise of a lot of little transistor radios.

"So what for God's sake happened?" Cox asked.

"He started leaving more and more stuff behind, that's what happened. He used to come on patrol with nothing on but a pair of shorts and nothing in his belt but a bayonet. Last I saw of him, he had started going into the fucking jungle by himself, stark buck-assed naked, with a knife in his teeth like Tarzan."

"The trouble with that story," Cox remarked, trying to keep the disappointment out of his voice—and he was very disappointed, because he had expected to learn something, and instead he had only heard something, "is that you can't tell exactly where it starts to be a lie."

"That's right," said Rellin, "that's exactly right. You can't, and I won't tell you. You just have to think about it for a while and figure out for yourself where the lie begins."

"I'll let you know," Cox said.

SIX

EARLIER THAT day, Track had measured the ground.

As best he could shape it up, the ideal sector for his field problem lay northeast of the bivouac area, where a clearly defined low plateau, spacious enough to accommodate a company and well enough supplied with earthworks to defend it, rose at the top of three gentle and thickly wooded slopes. The fourth side of the plateau crumbled away into a narrow river. He stood on the bank of the river, relaxed and abstracted, making notes inside the cover of a paperback copy of I. A. Richards' *Practical Criticism*.

It would be like marching across a chessboard.

Several days earlier, Headquarters, not too surprisingly, had turned the total execution of the problem over to him and the resources at his command. The resources at his command were his company. Period. There would be no formally designated Aggressor troops from the Special Forces unit assigned to the post, as he had hoped (just have two platoons stick white cockades in their sweatbands, lieutenant), no heavy weapons, no armed or armored vehicles, no artillery, and no air support. Only the company, split along its invisible middle, its hundred and eighty close and casual friends and foes designated at hazard deadly enemies each to each; their personal weapons, their boredom and their pride their only sustenance; their status taken as optimum in all respects. Such simplification was a form of cheating, just as his presence on this alien ground was a form of cheating, and he would have to deal with Melton's scorn at the orderly precision of the exercise. Well, that was all right. Track had a single black cloth bar sewn to the collar of his fatigue shirt, and Melton's scorn would have to be, finally, silent.

He looked at the notes he had taken inside the cover of his book. Back in his office the next day, he would work them out at greater length, he would translate words and numbers into Fortran IV, prime manner of speaking for his oiled sleek machine waiting with its charge of warriors' wisdom to turn the concentrated dream of his thesis into an item of the real world. The private war of Thomas Tallin Track, waged and written in a private language. He fitted the book back into his shirt pocket and permitted himself an empty moment in the cool still afternoon.

The river played below him, white and noisy at its edges, full of the weak energy of some final melting snow from a mountain too far away to see. The broken plain before him was silent perforce; since his choosing it, it had ceased to be a part of nature for things to live on and had become instead a waiting stage. The evergreens around it revealed a wind with their gently dancing branches.

He wished he had a girl with him. He thought that, if he had, he would chance being happened on by somebody and make love to her here by the river; well, fuck her, anyway. There were few things in life quite as pleasant as watching a girl undress outdoors, making a suburban woods a wilderness with an animal unleashing of body bare under the sky, spears of sun through trees, by running water.

Track shuddered. He had no girl here; he was alone. He settled his pistol belt more securely on his waist and started to walk back to the bivouac area. He would forget about the problem for a while, he would sit in his tent and feel central and useless, he would perform some satisfying minor chore, find some leather and buff it, perhaps he would clean his pistol.

But now he was swamped with an anger so tightly controlled that it would have found a way to be a rage in a man less mild. He sent for Melton.

"Was this your show?"

"Yes, sir."

"Who made up the ambush?"

"The platoon sergeants, sir."

That was clever. Track could hardly afford to show anger to all of his top NCOs, much less take action against them.

"First sergeant, you have pissed me off."

"Yes, sir."

"Pissed me off royally. Supremely. Is it your custom—" No, that was no good. He began again. "Are they back yet?"

"The patrol is back. The ambush isn't."

"Who did you put in charge?"

"Sergeant Cox, sir."

"You put an E-5 draftee over E-6 combat vets?"

The first sergeant hesitated. "It's just the way they decided to do it. It was more informal than that. Sergeant Cox had sort of talked over the idea with me, so I let him more or less run the thing."

"Report back to me with him when he gets in. That's all."

Melton was waiting at the perimeter when the platoon sergeants came out of the woods. He signaled Cox over to him.

"How'd it go?"

"OK. Most of these men will make good soldiers if they don't get lost in the science fiction."

97

"The architect of the science fiction wants to have a word with you. And me."

"Is he browned off?"

"Royally. Supremely."

"I'll tell him it was my idea."

They had been walking toward the CP. Melton stopped and put a hand on Cox's arm. "That's negative, sergeant. If the old man wants to hang somebody, he starts with the chain of command, just like you and me." He laced his fingers around his own throat. "One each neck and noose."

"I don't like it."

"You don't have to like it," Melton said fiercely.

"That's so."

He was no stranger to the pride in responsibility Melton was claiming. One might call it masochism if there were room for the gloomy borrowed word in the vocabulary of soldiering; to the two sergeants it meant nothing more than the other side of the coin of rank's privilege, and it was a surface no less gleaming. Only thus could the metal ring true.

A glance expressing this went between them, and then they looked away and dismissed it; not because they feared sentiment— that Cox was close to being Melton's son was too clear to be at issue or even of special interest—but because between men of taste the elaboration of virtues basic to their character is unattractive and unnecessary. They shared something that Lieutenant Track was not likely to know a great deal about—just honor, really. On the other hand, he did know a great deal about machines, and quite possibly that is a higher virtue just now.

Cox shrugged. "Shall I put zippers on my stripes?"

"Naw, that's all right. He's got a razor blade."

"Maybe I better put a zipper on my nuts."

Melton laughed. Some men never become comfortable enough

with themselves to loosen their laughter, but he was not one. Cox felt better.

"Those kids really reacted pretty well. It would be a shame if they had to start waiting for permission from the sweetheart of IBM every time it's lay-your-money-down."

"That's what this is all about."

At the CP tent, the two sergeants did not pause to exchange glances. Track was sitting behind his field table, polishing the lenses of his glasses with a bore-cleaning patch. Melton and Cox came sharply to attention and saluted.

"Sir, First Sergeant Melton and Sergeant Cox reporting to the company commander as ordered."

Track returned it. "At ease. Sergeant Cox, make your report."

Cox said promptly, "Sir, my ambush took successful action against your recon patrol. We sustained no casualties. Your patrol was destroyed." He paused. "If that's what you mean."

"What do you mean, if that's what I mean?"

"Sir, I'm not sure if you wanted a report on the progress of the action or on the—ah—the nature of the activities."

"Sergeant, the Army seems to have taught you as much governmentese in two years as it has Sergeant Melton in twenty. Congratulations."

Cox said nothing.

"Did I order that patrol to be ambushed?"

"Sir, I think—"

"Answer the goddam question!"

"No, sir."

"No, sir, what?"

"No, sir, you did not order the patrol to be ambushed."

"Who did?"

"Sir, First Sergeant Melton and I planned the ambush to—to see if the troops were on their toes."

99

"Is First Sergeant Melton the company commander?"

"No, sir."

"Are you the company commander?"

"No, sir."

"Who is?"

"You are, sir."

"Did I order that ambush?"

"No, sir."

"Did First Sergeant Melton have the authority to order the ambush without my knowledge?"

"I guess not, sir."

"You guess not?"

"No, sir, he did not."

"Do you?"

"No, sir."

Track, who had been watching his own fingers press the cotton over the lenses of his glasses in a tight little circle, stopped, and looked up for the first time. "Rest, gentlemen. And sit down."

"Sir," Melton began, "Sergeant Cox was following my instructions. If you're after somebody's ass—"

"I'm not after anybody's ass. At least I don't think I am. I'll be able to tell you better in a few minutes. Who led the patrol?"

"Private Pendleton, sir."

"And he fucked it up?"

"No, sir, not really. He managed all right."

"Shall I put him in for a Silver Star?"

"I'd like to put him in for pfc as soon as I can, sir." Cox said. "He was a sad sonofabitch when I first got hold of him, and he's come a long way."

"Where does the credit for that belong?"

"Well—I don't know, sir. I guess he finally just started getting his shit together."

100

"You know, I've looked at your record, Cox. You're one of the best young NCOs I've ever worked with."

"Yes, sir."

"Though you do seem to be in the habit of putting in repeated applications for transfer to a combat unit. Captain Hillock apparently saw fit to ignore them. I've been doing the same because I want you in my company."

"Yes, sir."

"I *don't* want you to play games with me. Not even to see if the troops are on their toes."

"Yes, sir."

"They almost were," First Sergeant Melton interposed softly. "You weren't."

Track glanced at him. "All right, that's all, Sergeant Cox. Dismiss."

After Cox had left, Track said to Melton:

"I'd better clear something up before we go much further. There's been a tacit agreement between us—"

Explicit, Melton thought.

"—that you would do the bits and pieces for the company and I would rubber-stamp it and do my own work my own way. But that does not extend to my underwriting your attempts to undercut me. I want you to tell me why you pulled this stunt. And—not incidentally—I want you to tell me why you think I'm not on my toes. And then I want you to tell me why you felt free to make that remark."

"Do you mind if I smoke?"

"Yes."

"Sir, I'm not trying to undercut you. I thought you might not regret having a—a graphic demonstration of how the unpredictable can foul up your plans."

"In combat, the possibility of an ambush is not unpredictable."

101

"That's like saying that in combat the possibility of death is not unpredictable. It don't help unless you know when and where," Melton countered.

"We'll let that go for the moment. What about your saying I wasn't on my toes?"

"Sir, I was out of line. I apologize."

"Very well."

"But you weren't. I'd like to say that now, in private. If I'm going to be of any use to you, lieutenant, I have to be able to speak freely."

"Permission granted. Proceed."

"Sir, assume that was an actual patrol. How is your computer going to help those men in the ten seconds from the time the ambush is sprung to the time when it closes over them completely?"

"For God's sake," said Track impatiently, "you're trying to push my conclusions to a point that looks logical but is in fact absurd. It's as though you were to ask me what the computer can do to help one man face-to-face with one enemy soldier. The answer is nothing. There is a point at which the variables become too many, the situation too fluid, and the action too fast. All I'm trying to do is redefine that point. I think I can bring it down to company level or lower. I never intended to cope with units as fragmented as patrols, or with individual personnel. The problem there is answered the way it has been since the first caveman picked up a stick."

"Yes, sir."

"But you know that. There's something else, isn't there?"

"I guess maybe there is."

The lieutenant relaxed visibly. He put his glasses back on, with careful cruelty fitting the metal rims against the red welts worn into either side of his nose. He pushed a tall green pack of Pall Malls across the tabletop. "Then let's hear it." He had no way of knowing that the offhand request had the effect of throwing the first sergeant on the mercy of his own image of his own cleverness, vividness, his secret cache of literacy and wit; now he might have to be Melton the epigrammatist, the draftsman of eloquent letters, dear Johns of death. The only other option was to open that core of himself which was wedded to the center of the idea of the Army, and he would not do that for a uniformed civilian whose weapons were neither idea nor flesh, but sediment from technology, which so often weds science to crime, which makes armies stronger and armed men weak.

Melton lashed about for images.

"Sir—"

And then, speaking the initial incantatory indispensable word, he realized for the first time in twenty years that every word that followed it would have to be in some measure, however small, a lie; and he almost despaired; and then the same twenty years rescued him.

"Sir, it's a little hard to explain. But it has to do with why I wanted Sergeant Cox to mount that ambush rather than one of the other men, who might have seemed better qualified."

"Go on."

"Sergeant Cox is a soldier. He's younger than a lot of his men, he's a draftee, he's got less time in the Army than plenty of privates, and he's never been in combat. But he's a soldier. He's a soldier the same way that—that—well, I don't know who to name." He did, though. Figures of antiquity, figures of the present made ancient by the stern chipped mantles of their *démodé* honor and resolve, drifted into his mind like marble busts. But he feared to sound foolish. He feared to come too close with the thing hidden in himself, the thing which you tarnish in the telling. "But I know he's a soldier. It's something I can tell."

"A soldier like you."

103

"A soldier like I tried to be when I was much younger. The way—"

"The way I, for example, am not."

"I think—I think that's right, sir."

"Go on."

Melton now took one of the cigarettes, but he did not light it; he played with it as though it were a pencil or a pointer for which he had some use in readiness. The gesture was the first clear loss of poise Track had ever witnessed in the man.

"Sir—what you told me a while back may be true. It may be that the wars of the future will have no more use for an infantryman. Maybe men in business suits will punch buttons and fend each other off with complicated bluffs. Maybe nobody will ever get killed again until we all get killed at once. That would be all right with me.

"But if they ever do need us again, like they needed us pretty bad not so damn many years ago, I don't like to think of a soldier —a real soldier—being tangled into all those complications— those deceptions. Am I making sense?"

"Not yet," Track answered, "but you may be headed that way."

"What I mean is . . . a man like Cox. He's not a murderer, not a killer, not any of that kind of civilian shit—"

"Are you sure?"

"—and he's not a politician. The—the—oh, Christ, the *moral* questions—"

"Never mind that. I accept that he's a soldier."

"He's more than just a soldier." Melton was suddenly excited, as though he had suddenly and finally found the image that would illuminate his thought. "He's a *warrior*."

Track smiled thinly. "All right, first sergeant. Now I see what you're talking about. You mean it's a shame they took von Richthofen out of his Fokker with his plume and spurs and seat-of-the-pants jousting and put him into an F-104 in a G suit with

104

a slide rule and some buttons to push at a target he'll be past before he sees it. Sorry about that, but I didn't design the twentieth century."

"No, and I'm not trying to romanticize it. At least I don't think I am. I just mean that a man like Cox has got some hard dark values within himself that have a right to be tested."

"They will be. My computer won't squeeze his trigger for him."

"It'll point his muzzle."

"So what? Look, I'm having a little trouble with your logic."

"It's not logic," said Melton miserably. "It's more than logic."

"For God's sake, do you want to fight wars by magic?"

Melton countered: "Has a man on foot ever fought them any other way?"

Track stood up. "Use your head. You think a computer-programmed fire fight is different from any other? It's different in only one respect. You're more likely to win it."

"That's not how it's different."

"The ultimate tendency of the crap you're talking would oblige you to say: do away with radios because they interfere with a trooper's moment of truth; trade rifles for spears because guns kill at a distance and you can't get a charge unless you work in close; don't use artillery because shells are too noisy and you must maintain a reverent quiet in the search for death. Jesus Christ!"

"No. Although . . ."

"Well?"

"What you say might be true," Melton finished, with the quiet simplicity of a man who no longer cares if he is branded mad. "Being a soldier is such a terrible thing that there is no salvation in it if what we do is lost in the things we do it with."

Track stared at him. Melton saw the fear of mystery seal over the officer's eyes, narrow and unquiet behind the thick lenses. If there had been any communion between them, it was now at an end. Melton felt fruitless and, feeling so, felt liberated. It is never easier to speak the truth than when you are sure it will go unrecognized.

"But that doesn't matter. That's not the difference. All our modern weapons may get us away from what we do, but they don't deny the probability of finding and recognizing the things in ourselves that make our actions possible. Let them be hideous, appalling; no doubt they usually are. But there is that other thing."

"Finish up," said Track roughly, "I have work to do."

"No, sir. You have machines to tend. *I* have work to do. But I will finish." Track's ear caught at last what his mind had not been supple enough to identify: the heavy formality of the missed contraction. The sergeant's speech had turned to writing; summation rode his tone. "The other thing is courage, which you once described to be as the combination of a man's health and humor and opinions and toilet training and a lot of other stuff that can be broken down and spit out by your computer in a description of how a man will react when his life is on the line. Sir, I don't know what courage is. But I've seen it. And it ain't that.

"If you send a man like Cox into battle with a computer on his back to make his choices for him, if you make him believe that his actions can be translated into their most petty terms, then he can never come face to face with his courage or his cowardice. He can never exhaust his will and see what lies beyond. *He cannot be a soldier.*"

"Sergeant, this is touching. I don't mean to be sarcastic. It really is. . . ."

"And if he is not a soldier, he will not fight well. And if he dies, there will be no meaning in it."

"There is no 'meaning' in death anyway," Track mocked.

"That is so," Melton said. "But there is meaning in the manner of it. Lieutenant, I told you I'm not trying to romanticize this. I have nothing against all these new systems of organizing the city of the Army. Let the computers order my laundry, process my files,

106

make out my pay check, punch my TS chit, let them develop grand strategies and big pictures to their heart's content. Even let them declare a war for me to fight in. But don't let them follow me right down to the wire and tell me how to die in it."

"Good Lord," the officer said at last, "your objection is . . . philosophical." He said the word as though wondering why it still remained in the language.

"Yes," Melton answered, "philosophical."

After a little while, Track said, "Is that all?"

"That's all."

"OK. Thank you. Now I want your promise, your oath, your guarantee . . . your word of honor that you will never work outside me or against me again. That you will follow orders. That you will make this company perform as I want it to perform. Clear?"

"Yes, sir."

"I have your word?"

"Yes, sir. You have."

"Very good. Dismiss."

Melton saluted.

"See if the guard is ready for inspection. Report to me." He returned the salute. Melton did an about-face. Track sat down again behind the table and resumed the cleaning of his pistol.

Sunday Pendleton had all of Sunday. He simply had it. The whole day, all of it, from the moment he awoke—not was awakened—until ten o'clock, 2200, when the lights went out and only sleep separated him from the new week. Ten o'clock Sunday night was a cheerless time, but at eight in the morning—and he could not sleep later no matter how hard he tried—the open day lay before him, infinitely long and green and so full of choices to be made and modest pleasures to be sampled that he hardly knew where to begin.

The first Sunday—back in basic, so many weeks ago—he had

107

been totally bewildered by a single hour of freedom. It followed days of unremitting strictures that had worn the corners of his personality smooth and all but eradicated his sense of self; so he had dutifully accompanied the insistent Young—who was some kind of improbable High Church Anglo-Episcopalian—to the post chapel for morning prayer, though he had not been inside a church since his fifteenth birthday. (His parents had much earlier set that as the cutoff date for his compulsory attendance, sure that long habit, compounded less of piety and ritual than of fondness for the strong hymn tunes of the communion and a haunted devotion to the rich cadences of the litany, would secure his faith. They had been wrong. No, they had just been not quite right.) On the outside, the chapel was another brick box like the rest of the post buildings, with a cross of unpainted I-beams jammed on the roof like an afterthought or an uncompleted asterisk; but inside it was white and gold and furnished tastefully and expensively with familiar objects which spoke of home and childhood in a way that bewildered him anew. Young actually genuflected toward the altar before moving into a pew—and there were pews, not folding chairs—and Pendleton remembered to grant at least a tentative nod to the empty cross before following his friend in.

The chaplain wore vestments, of course, but beneath the hem of his cassock Pendleton could see the yellow-striped blue trousers of an officer's dress uniform. Like most Episcopal priests, the chaplain had a mellow and convinced voice that seemed to make the artistry of the litany a personal possession being gingerly shared. Although almost ten years had passed since he had held a Book of Common Prayer, Pendleton found that he rarely had to glance at the page as he heard his voice mix into the low murmur of the small congregation. He kept looking around the inside of the chapel the same way Jonah looked around the inside of the belly of the whale. *Almighty and most merciful father, we have erred, and strayed from thy ways like lost sheep, we have followed*

108

too much the devices and desires of our own hearts, we have offended against thy holy laws, we have left undone those things we ought to have done and we have done those things we ought not to have done, and there is no health in us. There certainly wasn't much health in Pendleton, who had been suffering from three sorts of bronchial disruption since his first week in the Army, which, characteristically, had kept him smothering hot at night and put him to doing push-ups on ice puddles in the predawn chill.

While the organist began tampering with some Handel, he idly turned over the mimeographed weekly order of service that he pulled from the rack behind the pew in front of him. "Well, fuck me in the left ear," he whispered to Young, "look at that." On the cover was a handsome color photograph of the Tomb of the Unknown Soldier.

He did not return to chapel the next week, or ever again, but it wasn't really because of the bit of pornography he'd found in the pew. It was just that he had become more secure with his short freedom and wanted to make better use of it.

There seemed to him, then, to be so many different ways he could do so. He could put on his class A uniform and go to the snack bar for breakfast; he could *buy* his own breakfast and eat it and smoke a cigar at the table afterward without having some sergeant wander past and scream, "Eat up and get out! Whaddaya think this is, a fuckin' dayroom?" He could go to the service club and sit in one of the big chairs and read old magazines or put a dime in one of the typewriters and pound out thirty minutes' worth of letters before the thing locked itself up again. He could shoot pool. He could walk along a drill field under the autumn trees and frosted blue sky, scattering leaves, maybe even with his hands in his pockets, to the main PX and buy a candy bar. He could go to the movies if the post theater ever showed anything but *Penelope* or *Red Tomahawk*. He could go back to the snack bar and buy a flat preformed grease-caked hamburger for lunch, buy it with his own money, and then go sit in the service club again. He could do these things until ten o'clock at night, almost free of being accountable to someone, of the perpetual feeling of *being* accountable to someone, for every move, someone who would inevitably disapprove of whatever move it was.

That was Sunday, all day of it, fat, free and his.

He sometimes remembered with a sense of wonder that back when he was a civilian, he had been often bored, bored because he had nothing new or interesting to do. It seemed to him now that he must have been insane. It is not necessary to have anything to do; it is only necessary to have a space in your life where people are not doing things to you.

That was Sunday.

And this was Sunday. So Pendleton, awake at eight, rose and dressed and left the barracks quickly, for it is a cardinal rule that you do not remain in your company area when you are free to leave it. Technically, the day was his, and he could spend it sitting on his bunk or lounging in the dayroom if he so chose; but practically, there was always sure to be a sergeant or a surly Sp4 looking for a detail—"gimme five of you three mens!"—and common sense told him not to be where they were. In any case, he was sick of the squad bay, and he had learned early that trainees are allowed in their dayroom only to clean it.

So he split. He had his girl's most recent letter in his pocket, as yet unmemorized, and the luxury of the day stretched before him in which to endlessly reread and interminably answer it. He went to the snack bar and ate; and now, already, he had a choice to face: there were two service clubs he could go to. The more attractive was near the company. He settled for the other, a huge dark barn with a balcony around the top, the incessant rattle of pinball machines and the liquid squalling of two jukeboxes inside making a field of sound that was soon as comfortable as silence. *Dearest darling, enclosed find (in the better-late-than-never cate-*

*gory) one each pair authentic civilian (female type) pantyhose,
much the worse for wear, but maybe just right for your pur-
poses. . . .*

Did she know his purpose? Pendleton wondered. Would she
be shocked or did she seek her own lonely comfort? And when
the hell had she started wearing pantyhose? He thought with sick
longing of the presentation her body made in rust-colored stockings and rose-colored garter belt, all the bare white skin—or was
it flesh?—whiter and barer in the frame of lace and silk—O fool, I
will go mad—and was dismayed at the new development. Pantyhose were for sausages. Maybe these really were for his boots; no,
it was too late for that. . . .

Anyway, sent with love. I just wish my legs came with them—
He winced. There was something unattractive about that dis-
embodied image.

*—that all of me could come to you, but I don't suppose that
would do us much good in a room with seven other guys in it.*
Baby, you'd be amazed.

She went on with pert chatter about the routines her life had
settled into in his absence, her school, her friends, their friends,
movies, books: Manhattanville, hippies, lawyers, med students,
marginal fools and self-styled saints who dreamed of serf orchestras
sawing Haydn under Tolstoi's father's window; Fellini, Visconti,
Brook, all Westerns and most SF, Fowles, Hawkes and DHL, fuck
it all. He was both attracted and irritated. It seemed to him emi-
nently likely that there really was a world whose citizens had time
for things other than marching and cleaning and polishing and
running and being exhausted and invisible, but it also seemed
irrelevant. He wanted something significant to share, not these
implausible memories. He guessed he wanted to hear her bitch to
him about her drill sergeant as he bitched to her about his. Was
it possible she didn't have one?

—found this special exercise you mention very interesting but

111

not very clear. Do you carry around little Univacs or what? And are you going to be one of the good guys or one of the bad guys? Please enlighten. Please write. Please write right now, right? I love you. Me.

He wondered if she closed with the declaration as he did, out of duty. It didn't matter. He ("You only love me for my body!") only loved her for her body, that was for damn sure, and on that count he loved her so much that he felt weak and desperate thinking about it. *Dearest dear yourself (retch), your pantyhose have given both boots and low-quarters a lasting luster, and they haven't upset my stomach either, unlike most harsh washday products. The Good Conduct Medal will reach you shortly. I wish you were here too, so I could fuck your brains out, I am half crazy with missing you and all those fine fast times up against the dormitory wall with the nuns peeping from the high windows to make sure you didn't perform any but the milder perversions. And I surely miss our long discussions of Plato, too, kid. The operation is the brainchild of our new CO, who comes to us straight from MIT or someplace like that, and who is going to revolutionize land warfare, or anyway keep himself amused while he's putting in his time, which I for one don't blame him for a bit. All it amounts to is an ordinary infantry field problem, jazzed up a little with this electronic brain to tell us where the bad guys are and when to shoot them. The bad guys are the first and second platoons of the company, who will be trucked to the problem area to dig in sometime tomorrow. The other two platoons will march out there tomorrow afternoon, we'll victoriously take the position with the aid of Captain Track's computer and our funny little rifles, and then we'll all come back and find something else fun to do on Tuesday. Rest assured that your true love intends to perform with conspicuous valor, even to the laying down of his life. Could they ask for more? (And rest assured that your true love would a whole*

112

lot rather be in your pants than in the boonies, but England ex-
pects, etc.)

He wrote pages and pages more. But the mocking tone did not falter, the tone that showed all too clearly he was writing to his pussy, not his queen. It would dismay her. She would have no way of knowing that for him to open his heart now would be to show how much of it had begun to belong to the Army, any being much. Then he wrote:

You write too.

I love you.

SEVEN

AT 0530 on Monday morning, when dawn was nothing more than a pencil line of yellow drawn neatly the whole length of the flat eastern horizon, Track met in his office with his NCOs. The company was at morning chow. Its barracks, which filled the view from the lieutenant's window, were brightly lighted, but no one was visible in the rooms except the barracks orderlies, who could be seen on each of the three floors, slow sleepy figures in T-shirts and fatigue pants standing dully in the centers of the clean shining rooms, motionless and purposeless, like very old men in homes for the senile, who stand quietly in the centers of their rooms, watching the arrival of dawn and twilight.

Cox was the first to enter the empty room. He left the light off, went to the window, and looked across to the barracks at the floor where his platoon lived. All the sashes were raised and lowered six inches at bottom and top. The venetian blinds were pulled up, their slats at an equal angle, their cords hanging straight. At inspection this morning, he would pick up each cord and look in the plastic bell on the end for dust or lint or fuzz, and sweet Jesus help the squad leader in the room where he found it.

This kind of thing was known by the troops as harassment. They could understand the practical necessity for having your living

117

quarters clean, your latrines spotless; but it was precisely beyond these necessities that Cox wanted to go. His minute inspections were no more harassment than was the burden on a monk to answer the morning bell. They were pure demonstrations of power and order; they affirmed place and logic and design. This is the Army, Cox said silently with his hard inspections, the only land left in America where you must be perfect in social small detail. Here it matters most to be clean, sharp and squared away just where it matters least.

But the men still called it harassment. Most of them were not very religious.

Cox snapped on the light. Specialist Reynolds came in from the orderly room and offered him a cup of coffee—"with the first sergeant's compliments."

"My compliments to the first sergeant and tell him thank you, two lumps, no cream."

"Yes, sir, Sergeant Cox. Will the platoon sergeant have a plain or frosted doughnut, platoon sergeant?"

"Get the fuck out of here, Reynolds."

"On my way, sergeant."

"Where's the old man?"

"The lieutenant is out in the parking lot wiping the come off his bucket seats, platoon sergeant. He is sorry to keep you waiting."

Cox eyed the clerk. He was clean, sharp, and squared away; something of a snob and a fool; and, as company clerk, rather powerful in the small ways that characterize the civilian comforts of military life. He was first to see orders and directives, he always knew where everybody was, and he could make out passes and such, juggle KP lists; it was wise to have him for a friend. Cox would not have disliked him but for that reason.

He ignored Reynolds, took a chair by the lieutenant's desk, looked around the office. The severe lines of the metal furniture and the flat ugly institutional shades of the paint had been softened

118

by a rug and a few small wooden tables, by framed prints hung symmetrically around the walls. The print over Cox's chair depicted a soldier with a carbine, crouched under a log, jackboots moving past his hidden head, his features shaded and intense. The legend below it read:

I WILL NEVER SURRENDER OF MY OWN FREE WILL. IF IN COMMAND, I WILL NEVER SURRENDER MY MEN WHILE THEY STILL HAVE THE MEANS TO RESIST.

Cox noticed that the print that hung over the computer terminal read:

I WILL NEVER FORGET THAT I AM AN AMERICAN FIGHTING MAN, RESPONSIBLE FOR MY ACTIONS, AND DEDICATED TO THE PRINCIPLES THAT MADE MY COUNTRY FREE. I WILL TRUST IN MY GOD AND IN THE UNITED STATES OF AMERICA.

The other platoon sergeants came in together and said good morning to him. Then Lieutenant Track came in, followed by Melton, and they all stood until he waved them back into their seats.

Track looked tired. If his fatigues were crisp, the body inside them seemed worn and in some need of pressing. He had been up all night, and his eyes were lit with Benzedrine. He sat down behind his desk.

"Relax, gentlemen, please. Smoke if you like. If anybody else wants coffee, I'll give Reynolds a yell." He did not speak again until the ritual of serving had been accomplished, glossing the meeting—as it seemed to Melton, who had remained standing behind the lieutenant's chair—with the politesse of a tea party.

"You're probably all wondering why I called you here." Track went on without leaving a space for the formal laughter his rank entitled to the aged line. "I won't keep you too long. I don't intend to go into too much detail now, but the company clerk will

119

be giving you mimeographed instructions and contour maps and such on the way out. Actually, I *can't* tell you too much, because a lot of these details are going to be worked out by you—in action —and I don't want to know anything about them until they come up.

"I've discussed some of the—ah—theory of this thing with Sergeant Melton, but all I'm going to go into with you is the nuts and bolts." He paused to light a cigarette. The fluorescent glare above him thinned the smoke into planes of gray light. "OK, here it is. This is day one—there won't be a day two—of an exercise I am calling Operation Doublethink. In this exercise, two platoons of this company will hold a defensive position now designated as Hill 115. Obviously, I won't point that out on the map, because the attacking company is not to know where the hill is. Beforehand.

"The other two platoons will attempt to take the position.

"We will in all cases be using only indigenous equipment and personnel. The first and second platoons are now designated as Aggressor Force, and will hold the hill. Sergeant Melton will be in command of the force. Third and fourth platoons, under the immediate command of Sergeant Sherman, are now designated as the Company, and will be the attacking party. There will be umpires from Battalion HQ to observe the progress of the action. Are there any questions at this point?

"All right. Aggressor Force has had the necessary uniform modifications made"—and Cox noticed for the first time that Rellin and Disenhaus had crimson tabs on the collars of their fatigue shirts, and large crimson triangles taped to the front of their helmet liners— "and will be inspected by me in that uniform at the 0630 formation. After noon chow, Aggressor Force will be trucked to the hill to take up whatever defensive position its commander sees fit. Sergeant Melton?"

"Sir."

"Within the stated limits, you may arm and equip your unit as you wish, without my further knowledge. I have given orders to that effect."

"Yes, sir."

"Later this afternoon, the Company will road-march to the hill and attempt to effect its capture, through the destruction or seizure of the Aggressor Force. As I have indicated, the field first sergeant will be in command. He will be in constant radio contact with me here, in this office. I will direct his operations with the aid of the computer.

"Questions."

"Sir."

"Sergeant Rellin."

"Sir, what about artillery and air support?"

"There will be none."

"How do we handle combat intelligence? I mean, do we send scouting parties? Do we know these people are up there, or do they ambush us, or what?"

"All of that is up to you. You know whatever you find out. I will indicate a line of march for the Company. Somewhere along it you will encounter the Aggressor. It's up to you how you prepare for and handle the situation."

"This is still pretty much a textbook operation, isn't it, sir?" Sergeant Sherman murmured. "I mean, the forces are equal in almost all respects and we both know roughly what to expect. The element of surprise is minimal."

Track sighed. "That's true as far as it goes. But, gentlemen, what I'm working with here is an idea in its infancy. All you need to know is that I'm trying to find out how closely and how well a computer can perform with a small line unit in a rapidly changing combat situation. The intelligence you mention, Sergeant Rellin, is of paramount importance. All I will know before the action is who's fighting, and where. Everything else I will have

121

to work with as it develops, as it gets back to me. And precisely because we have a pat situation overall, I want maximum possible flexibility and realism in small detail. When this thing is over, I want every man in it—combat vets included—to feel like he's been in a battle."

"Thank you, sir."

"Any further questions? Then I thank you, gentlemen. Leaders of Aggressor Force are dismissed. Your troops will fall out for inspection at 1030 sharp; you may give them the time between to prepare for that. Check with Specialist Reynolds for the handouts. You other sergeants keep your seats."

Cox looked at his watch. It was 0550. The sun was up.

"Fall in!"

But it had not warmed the air. Now the entire company was outside the barracks, in fatigues, baseball caps and under arms, and threads of breath were visible around the men's faces. Aggressor Force wore its red collar tabs and glowered festively at the Company, who glared benignly back. Holiday was in the air, for soldiers out of combat spend most of their time hiding from manual labor, and now a peaceful war had come to be a game for them, a sport, a diversion. They huddled together on their plot of ground, exchanging cigarettes and threats of doom, done with going through the motions of police call, feigning tommy guns and karate turns like boys with water pistols in a summer alley. Chow formation was past, now there was this formation, later today there would be others. In the Army, formations occur often enough to sap the shape of the duty day. No one cares unless it is very cold or very hot or very wet. Men in the middle can almost sleep.

"Fall in!"

"Fall in means fall in *at attention,* young man!"

122

"Wake up! Wake up!"

"Squad leaders," Cox said, "*re*port."

"First squad present 'counted for."

His turn: Pendleton saluted, Cox returned it. "Second squad present."

"Third squad present."

"Fourth squad present or accounted for, sergeant."

"I don't like 'accounted for,'" Cox said, "I like 'present.' Young, where are your men?"

"Desalo in hospital, Tally on KP, sergeant."

"Westrop?"

"Two men sick call, sergeant."

"This day," Cox said, "this day of days." If it were possible, he was more immaculate than usual. He had sprayed his helmet liner with silicone, and he was wearing his oldest, most faded and therefore most classy fatigues, all crease and no wrinkle, starched beyond any resemblance to cloth.

From Sherman, standing before the company:

"P'toon sergeants—*re*port!"

Disenhaus, Rellin, Iacone and Cox pivoted toward him, saluting in turn:

"First platoon present 'counted for—"

  "Second platoon present 'counted for—"

    "Third platoon present 'counted for—"

      "Fourth platoon present 'counted for—"

Sherman did an about-face and was looking at Track. He saluted.

"Sir, company present for inspection."

Track returned it. "Give them parade rest, sergeant."

Sherman turned back to the rectangle of men.

"Company!"

"Platoon!"

"P'toon!"

"——toon!"

"——n!"

"Parade—*rest!*"

"All right," Track said. "At ease."

He granted them a moment to settle into the illusion of relative comfort.

"All right, listen up. Today, as you know, is something of a special day in our training. The field exercise you are about to . . . embark upon is ordinary enough in itself, but it has a new aspect that is a little unusual. Practically speaking, this will not have a measurable effect on any of you except the NCOs and the squad leaders, but I want all of you to know a little about what is going on. I might start by saying that if this exercise comes off the way I want it to, there are going to be three-day passes floating out of the orderly room like confetti on a big parade, and if it doesn't, I am going to be kicking more ass than a bull in a pasture. Are you with me so far?"

"Yes, sir!"

"I can't hear you."

"*Yes, sir!*"

"Are you gonna do the job?"

"*Yes, sir!*"

"Do it right?"

"*Yes, sir!*"

"That's affirmative. You are. Now here's what's happening. Most of you are probably aware that I have in my office a funny little machine which I play with whenever I get a little free time. Well, gentlemen, this afternoon, when you are engaged on that exercise I spoke of, I'm going to be asking that funny little machine some questions, and when it gives me back the answers, I'm going to be able to tell the Company exactly how to neutralize the Aggressor Force."

124

Pendleton whispered to Young, in front of him, "I think the lieutenant is underestimating the intelligence of the American fighting man."

Cox was about to speak, but Track beat him to it. "You have a question there, soldier?"

"No, sir, no question."

"You want to let us all hear what's so funny?"

"Sir, excuse me. I was just saying how interesting it will be to see how the computer works in the exercise."

"Well, I'm glad you're interested, trooper. Thank you."

"Give me twenty, shithead," Cox said.

Pendleton shrugged and went down for the push-ups. Lieutenant Track droned on. Pendleton heard him saying: *luck, conduct, obey, information, sharpness, prepare, all respects, response, mission, find, fix, fight, finish, the real McCoy.* The computer did not seem to be changing things so very much.

Now Aggressor Force was gone. The Company had watched from its windows as the files of their enemy swung into the backs of the covered deuce-and-a-halfs, pulling each other up with their rifles in the proper way. The men were in full field gear; there actually seemed to be an alien, almost impressive, air about them, as though the new markings on their collars and helmets had in fact effected a change in allegiance to some dark and secret flag of an unknown state.

First Sergeant Melton, waiting at the head of the small column in his command jeep, had been designated a captain of Aggressors. He had been supplied with black felt captain's bars fixed to the red tabs and triangle on his uniform. His men, reporting, saluted. Track had laughingly remarked, on dismissing him from their final conference, "Now you outrank me." But Melton had always known that.

By 1100, the column was moving down the company street, the

125

insignia on its vehicles painted over with the red triangle, and that smeared with mud, the tops of the trucks daubed with camouflage, their intervals slowly widening in the slow pace of a tactical march. The antennae of the command jeep whipped smoothly in the wind. Five truckloads of men followed it. Behind them, another three trucks filled with mortars and machine guns, the newly designed blank ammunition, and supplies pulled into line. Each item of this equipment had been specifically called for by the computer on the basis of the minimal information Track had earlier read into it.

He stood in the doorway of his headquarters, watching the short column pass by. He saluted Melton solemnly, then called cheerfully, "We're gonna wipe you out!" He was still very tired, and there was the rest of the hard long day before him, but he was starting to feel exuberant. If this day was not precisely the summit of his career, it still was going to mark the pragmatic authentication of his theory, put a stamp of purpose on his military experience, be another line of litany in the wedding of an old art and a new science. Melton would find he was not the only philosopher of war.

"Good luck," Track called. "You'll need it."

The lieutenant, Pendleton noticed from his second-story window, stood in the doorway for a long time after the street was empty.

"Don't you have anything to do, young man?" Cox asked. He had come into the room as silently as rubber on glass.

"Uh . . . yes, sergeant."

"Then I suggest you get to it. If you don't have anything to do, we can find something for you, you can bet your sorry wilted hammer on that." He looked down at Pendleton's bunk, whose tightness had been stretched shapeless under the litter of field gear the soldier was preparing: pack and suspenders, helmet and liner, protective mask, pistol belt, canteen and first-aid pouch, ammuni-

126

tion cases, and a rifle and a bayonet with its scabbard—for the whole company had drawn their weapons from the arms room that morning.

Cox picked up the scabbard, unlocked it and carefully slid the bayonet out. A veil of Cosmoline lay under his gaze over the steel, which glimmered softly beneath it, like treasure seen under clear green water.

"You want to get all this shit off of here," Cox told him, "else it'll pick up grit and such when you're in the boonies." The remark, like nearly everything Cox ever said to one of his soldiers, was both a teaching and an order; but there was some vagrant harmony in his tone that made it seem almost conversational as well. The note was distinct enough to make Pendleton pause, assure himself with a glance at Cox's face that he had not misheard, and search for a civil reply: *How do you like the weather, when do we move out, you're too bright to be a lifer, got a girl back home, sarge?*

"Right, I'll do that. Ah . . . you got a light, sergeant?"

"Do I look like I light cigarettes for privates, private?" He offered a box of matches.

"Thanks. Ah . . . Sergeant Cox: what do you think about this thing of the lieutenant's?"

"Thing?"

"Idea. The thing in his office. The computer."

"I don't think much of anything about it. It's just another weapon."

"I'm not sure," Pendleton said, "I'm not sure that's all it is. What does the first sergeant think?"

"What does the first sergeant think?" Cox mocked. "What does Mr. Track think? What do I think? Have you got enough room in your head for thinking about all that and still getting your work done?"

"I guess I have enough for my small head thinking what a big

127

head everyone must have since everyone has such a big thought."

"That sounds like a quote from a book."

"It is."

"Pendleton, are you happy in the Army? Have you found a home in the Army? Do you like your work?"

"My work doesn't require much thinking, sergeant."

"And that's what you like to do? Think?"

"I guess so. I'm not very good at anything else."

"No? Would it interest you to know that you're not the absolutely rock-bottom worst soldier I've ever seen? Close to it, maybe, but not the worst?"

Pendleton said, "Sergeant Cox, if I'm turning into an adequate infantryman, I can't honestly say I'm happy about it."

"OK, thinker. But don't forget that only a very small part of your munificent pay goes to you for thinking. I would judge maybe somewhere between four-fifty and five dollars a month. And now the lieutenant has something in his office to do all your thinking for you." He snapped the bayonet sharply back into its scabbard and tossed it on the cot. "Don't kill anybody with that thing today, young man."

"I'd never kill anybody with it any day," Pendleton said bitterly.

Cox wanted to hit him. He said:

"That's not the way you played it on the close-combat course." He was unable to altogether erase from his voice the disappointment that would make Pendleton feel valued.

"That was different," Pendleton said, with uncharacteristic stupidity.

"Different. How?"

"It's hard to explain."

"Try. Try for Jesus."

"You made me," Pendleton said. "You ordered me to."

"I ordered you to kill a dummy. In combat, I would be ordering

128

you to kill a man. There is no difference. That's what giving an order means."

"Choosing to disobey makes a difference."

"That's so. Court-martial in training, death in combat. How do you like those flowers?"

"Sergeant Cox," Pendleton said, "I tried to tell you once. I can't kill a man like that. With a bayonet. And I'll tell you something else. I don't think you could either." Pendleton was pleading: though killing be condoned, let blood agony be condemned.

"So you're one of those, you simple little shit? You could jerk a lanyard on a howitzer to drop HE on an enemy you can't see, or maybe you could fire a rifle at a little toy shaped like a man three hundred yards away, but you wouldn't be nasty enough to get next to somebody whose breath you could smell and stab him, would you? You think there's a difference, don't you, thinker?"

Pendleton chanced, "I didn't mean to hurt your feelings."

"You didn't hurt my feelings, sonny. But if you're a thinker, you better start doing some hard thinking about who you are and where you are."

"I didn't ask to be here," Pendleton said.

Cox turned away. At the door he paused. "You are here, though, aren't you?" he said.

"Fall in!"

The two platoons that were the Company fell in. Before them lay a march, by truck and foot, of some few hours, with a mock battle waiting beyond it. Mock ammunition rested in the pouches on their belts, grenades filled with smoke instead of metal hung from their shoulder straps, tangles of weeds reshaped their helmets, grease darkened their faces. Pendleton's gear felt heavy to him already, just standing there, and that depressed him.

"Squad leaders—*re*-port."

129

"P'toon sergeants—*re*-port."

"Company!"

"P'toon!"

"——oon!"

"*Rest.*"

"All right, people, listen up," Track said. Pendleton found a weak joke in his tired mind and, with it, taste enough to let it fail to find expression: they had been listening up forever. Did no one ever listen down?

He gave them their final instructions. They involved fortune, behavior, obedience, knowledge, alertness, readiness, aspects, reaction, job, the mission of the infantry, the real thing. Pendleton wondered how much longer he could listen to military rhetoric; it was unbearable; no, that wasn't true, it was bearable for exactly one year, seven months and twenty-three days longer.

Track finished, exchanged salutes with Sergeant Sherman and walked swiftly away.

"Third platoon!" Sherman shouted, "Column of twos from the left—"

"Forward!"

                    "Stand fast!"

"—march!"

Pendleton put one foot in front of the other. Somewhere it has been recorded truly that all journeys begin so.

Although it would be at least three hours before the company made contact, Track went at once to his empty office and began waiting. He was too excited to do anything else. He should have gone to the O Club for a quiet beer, or at least done some paper work, but he didn't even try to. There was no one in the office to witness his exhilaration, so he made no effort to repress it. He sat down behind his desk and waited, for Haslip to call down from Battalion, for the Company to radio in.

Before him lay charts and graphs and sheets of figures. On one side of the desk sat the orderly-room coffee urn, and on the other a field radio which had been dismounted from his jeep and installed here with its battery. On the terminal, the code that gave him access to his section of the computer core had long since been dialed, and the receiver was resting in its holder above the keyboard. The computer's memory banks had been given exhaustive information about the company, statistical breakdowns of its size and strength and all quantifiable capacities, even a modest tangled try at turning its courage into numbers—and is that really so strange in a separate world where everything is done by the numbers?—but about the Aggressor Force it as yet knew nothing. It did know the Company was moving into hostile territory, and it knew the lay of the land the enemy waited on.

That enemy would be there, and in position, now.

At 1630, the Company radioed in. It had halted its march at the edge of the bivouac area, and was sending out a patrol. Thirty minutes later, the patrol made contact and took a prisoner.

Inside the back of the deuce-and-a-half, it was dark. The sun on the canvas had warmed the truck comfortably, and the dirt road unfolded behind the flapping arc over the tailgate like a receding tunnel. The truck behind them held steadily, a bit too close perhaps, showered with broken light from the bending trees above.

Pendleton sat by the tailgate, across from Young, his rifle between his knees with his helmet over its muzzle. The noise of the truck motor placed a continual soft pressure against his inner ear, like the wash of surf, and the jolting and shaking of the big vehicle made sleep an at best remote possibility. Young shouted across to him:

"What is the spirit of the bayonet?"

"Uh . . . love? Peace? Flowers?"

131

"Yeah, something like that. I'm proud of you, young soldier. You learn fast."

"Thank you, sir."

"I've got my eye on you."

"What?"

It was too noisy for banter. Pendleton was hungry. He drank a little water from his canteen. Putting it back into the case on his hip subtly rearranged the rest of his gear from the almost comfortable position he had finally found for it. His pack slipped lower and dug against his back. The truck hit a bump, and the wooden slats of the bench he was sitting on dipped away and rose sharply into his thighs.

"It's such a comfort to take the bus," Young said. Then they turned sharply and stopped. The driver cut the motor. Pendleton saw the truck behind them begin pulling over.

Now empty of mechanical sound, the silence filled with the lesser voices of the woods: birds, insects, the rustle of sycamore and saw grass. Cold commenced to come back into the dim blue day.

"Everybody outa the trucks!"

"Hit it! Let's go, let's go!"

Pendleton undid the chain on his side of the tailgate and kicked the tailgate free, watching the upside-down slats marked NOT TO BE USED AS TROOP LADDERS slam noisily against the body of the truck. He jumped off, banging his knee with his helmet. He saw Cox over by the next truck, swinging his clenched fist above his head in the "assemble on me" sign. Pendleton assembled on him.

"Put your goddam helmet on, troop! P'toon—*fall in!* At ease. Keep your canteens on your asses and your cigarettes in your pockets and your mouths shut."

Sfc Sherman, the field first, company CO—was he supposed to

132

be an officer now, or what?—came over, and Cox saluted him.

"Sergeant, we hoof it from here. You will go in advance of the weapons platoon when we move out. That'll be after your patrol gets back. Send 'em out now."

"Right, sir." Not too surprisingly, Cox next said, "Pendleton, fall out and fall in on me." A moment later he said softly, "All right, you know how this is played. Just like the last time. Take your squad. I'll give you a radioman. Watch your intervals, watch the trees, watch for smoke. Watch everything. Use your nose. You can even think if you want to."

"Yes, sergeant."

"Don't engage, and don't let anybody get caught, and don't lose anybody. Probe one thousand meters and flank back. What I want is a prisoner, if possible."

"A prisoner," Pendleton said stupidly.

"Yeah, you know, a bad guy. They'll have pickets out, or listening posts, or something. Pick one of 'em up. I don't want you near the main position—you wouldn't get that close anyway unless they're really asleep at the switch." He thought about Melton, commanding the Aggressor Force. "And they won't be."

"OK, sergeant."

"Get your men together and move out. Send me somebody for the radio."

Pendleton took his men off the trail as soon as they were away from the trucks. He had remembered to inspect each man's gear and weapons and to give his instructions before they left the area; now he made a radio check. Then they struck into the trees, heading northeast, so far apart that they were only just in sight of each other—though Pendleton kept the radioman close to him.

Movement was not easy. Deep in the forest, it soon became much darker and greener and cooler than it had been on the trail. There were twigs and branches scattered thickly underfoot,

133

making it necessary for them to sacrifice either speed or silence; to the squad leader's nervous ears, it seemed they were too often sacrificing both.

He felt a certain desperation. The enemy, in whatever strength, would be noiselessly waiting in some point of vantage: the tangle of the forest was not dense enough to work against both sides. He kept moving his head, watching for a glint of metal though he knew the Force's weapons would be dulled with tape or cloth, listening for steps or voices though he knew they would belong only to his own patrol.

A voice said, "Blackjack."

He looked at his watch. They had been gone for just under fifteen minutes, and covered no great distance; but now the bramble seemed to be thinning. His next few careful steps brought him to the edge of a creek so narrow that the crowd of grasses on either side almost roofed it over. Beyond the creek, with their backs to him, sat two soldiers. They had a radio, a light machine gun and a deck of cards. The cards kept slapping down with little snaps on an ammunition case between them. It seemed incredible that they had not heard him; but no, the tiny creek was whispering over its stones with a noise like that of wandering dry leaves or even footsteps.

His radioman had frozen; he had seen them too. *But this could be real*, Pendleton thought, looking at their backs, and at what he could see of their bored abstracted faces. *They could be my enemy. I could be theirs, they should be more careful.* Moving his head slowly as though he feared his neck might make a noise, Pendleton looked to his rear. He could see two more members of his squad moving forward, low-crawling slowly on their bellies, and he knew they had seen also, or had been signalled by Linton, the radioman; the radioman was down too; Pendleton felt like a fool that he should remain standing. He stepped back slowly and went down behind the wide trunk of an old elm. Now they would

134

hear him; but the slapping, the tapping of cards continued. He heard one of the men say, "Hit me, motherjumper," not very quietly.

They would have to be taught to play the game.

Pendleton worked his way back to where Linton and the other two men lay assembled and concealed and sealed together like a pact.

He whispered, "Remember we want a prisoner. We'll shoot the man who's closest to the radio. If he gets time to use it, our ass is in big trouble."

"You want to wait for the rest of the patrol?"

"That's negative. They may make more noise coming in. And we can't afford to wait for those guys to maybe see them first."

"I wish I could get all excited about this," said Linton.

The four men clicked off the safeties on their rifles and began to crawl forward. The edge of the creek offered no protection, no cover; Pendleton was simply going to have to simultaneously cover a mental and physical distance that would breed the judgment of when to act. He waited a little long. The card players, finally, heard them, and turned. Their machine gun, its muzzle up and north, was of no immediate use to them, but one of the men wasted time going for it anyway, and the other lunged toward the radio. Pendleton brought his rifle up to his cheek and fired a short burst, the other three men just ahead of or behind him. The four automatic rifles punched scores of the new plastic bullets into the area, and the Aggressor radioman gave a surprised shout. "Cocksucker—hold up! That shit stings, man!" The patrol jumped the creek, rifles at high port, just like a war movie. The Aggressor radioman's uniform was splattered across the legs and chest with vivid red splashes of warm plastic, now cooling and congealing into flaky puddles brown as old blood. He was nursing a welt on his left hand, bitching and complaining bitterly, and it was pretty clear that he was dead.

135

"Goddam, man, what if you hit somebody in the *eyes* with that shit? That shit *hurts*, man!"

"You ain't supposed to aim at people's faces," one of Pendleton's men told him.

"Well, Jesus Christ, you guys aimed it at every motherfucking square inch over here. How do you know—"

"You weren't hit in the eyes, were you?" Pendleton demanded, "so shut up. Bring the prisoner over here."

"I'm afraid we don't have a prisoner. Check this."

The other Aggressor grinned and closed his eyes and let his head slump forward to welcome his death. There were two plastic splashes over his stomach.

"Jesus Christ," said Pendleton, "who the fuck did that?"

"Get bent. You might of done it yourself."

"He ain't dead. He's just a little gut shot."

"*Dammit*," Pendleton said. "Listen, where's your main force, you Commie rat?"

"I'm dead," the Aggressor said. "Anyway, I don't speak English."

"You're not dead yet, you're just dying. Answer the goddam question."

"I can see my whole life passing in front of my eyes."

Pendleton put the muzzle of his rifle under the man's chin. "You're gonna see your teeth pass before your eyes if you don't start talking."

"You'd better get that fucker away from my face," the man said quietly. Pendleton did.

"Well, come on," the Aggressor said. "Let's get back to your lines so I can get some sack time."

Pendleton considered. There was no way of knowing who had heard the firing, but it was almost certain someone had—another outpost, or they might even be close to the main post itself. Or it

136

might be time for these people to be relieved, or to check in. Any way you cut it, they could not stay here.

There was no umpire in sight.

Pendleton tugged at the patch of plastic on the man's shirt.

"Hey, what you doin'?"

"I'm resurrecting you, baby."

"Man, you can't do that!"

"Fuckin' stuff won't come off. Somebody give me a lighter."

"You can't *do* that."

Pendleton touched the tip of the flame to the hardened plastic. It began to redden and then to melt, dripping away from the shirt like blood. He was able to get most of it off like that, and the rest largely yielded to the point of a bayonet.

"Now you aren't dead anymore," Pendleton said simply.

"I'll be damned if that's so!"

"You're a prisoner," Linton said. "We never touched you."

"You guys don't play fair."

"Look," said Pendleton wearily. "Lieutenant Track wants us to win. If we do, everybody gets good times. If we don't, he kicks ass. Why don't you wise up?"

"I'll be goddamned if I'm a prisoner," the man said stubbornly. "I'm dead, and the dead don't rise and tell no tales."

"Throw all their crap in the creek," Pendleton said. "Not the machine gun. They can carry that back with them."

The Aggressor radioman said, "All I can say is, you better hope nobody hits you on the skin with these neat new blanks. These fuckers *hurt*."

They tied the prisoners' hands. They made the undead man carry the machine gun with his hands tied to the barrel. Entirely untroubled by his deception, Pendleton collected the rest of his people, who had been converging on the sounds of battle, and led his patrol rapidly back to the company.

137

"That's very good work," Cox said.

"It'd be a lot better work if I wasn't dead!"

"Is this man dead?"

"He might have been wounded a little," Pendleton admitted.

"Sergeant Cox, I'd just like to make a little speech to your men if I may," the Aggressor radioman was saying. "I'd just like to tell them to be careful with these new blanks that aren't blanks, because you can really fuck somebody up with them. I'm damned if I know how they ever got authorized. I'm all in favor of some really first-class combat training—hell, there's nothing I like better —but I think maybe there ought to be a little more distinction made between this and the real thing. Seems to me—"

"Shut up," Cox said. "I *know* you're dead. You get along over there." He indicated a staked-off area near the cluster of trucks. "That's for casualties. You need anything, just tell a guard. You can sit on your ass for the rest of the day. You're a lucky man."

The Company had been shaped into a loose defensive position in the time the patrol had been gone. Pendleton could see the men grouped into their squads, away from the trucks; there were guards and two machine guns facing into the woods. Sfc Sherman was coming toward them.

"Sergeant, my man here got you your prisoner. Also captured a machine gun, killed an Aggressor and took no casualties."

"Good," said Sherman briefly. He glanced at the prisoner. "Get everything you can out of him. Don't be too long. Let me know when you're done."

Cox saluted.

"OK, Mr. Pendleton, let's take this gentleman over to where we can have some privacy."

"In the first place," the Aggressor said, "I'm dead and it's illegal for you to question me. Not to mention pointless. I want to see an umpire. In the second place, even if I weren't dead, all

138

I'd have to give you is my name, rank, service number and date of birth."

"That's true," said Cox, "but it happens we aren't interested in that information. What we're going to do is just step over here where we won't be in anybody's way and have a cigarette and a little chat. I'm going to give you a map, and you're going to mark it for me with the positions of your main force, outposts and the like. Then you're going to give me pretty much of a rundown on your troop placement, weapons positions, that sort of thing. In other words, you're gonna tell me everything I want to know."

The Aggressor stared at Cox, speechless. His hands had been untied from the machine gun and tied behind his back, and Cox and Pendleton had led him, not ungently, over to a stand of evergreens, and they now stood behind the trees, obscured from the view of the Company.

"Goddammit," said the prisoner, "how many times do I have to tell you I'm dead? This sonofabitch shot me and then peeled the goddam plastic glop off my shirt. Jesus, you fuckin' guys want to have your cake and eat it too."

"Here's the map," Cox said.

"How the hell can I mark a map with my hands tied behind my back? And anyway, I ain't gonna do it."

"Just tell me where. I'll mark it."

"I said I ain't gonna do it!"

Cox took out a pack of Luckies and lighted one for the prisoner.

"Now," he said, "fact is, you *are* gonna do it. So the question simply reduces itself to how. I would say that, basically, you have two possible ways. One is the easy way, and the other is the hard way. Now the easy way has got a lot to recommend it. In this way, we simply sit here and have a little talk. Then you get your hands untied and you get to go sit around in our POW compound for the rest of the day and bullshit with your dead buddy. Plenty of coffee and food and cigarettes."

139

Pendleton was looking away and listening closely to Cox's voice. It was slow and patient, and moving within it was a leaden stream of menace that could hardly have been more pronounced if this man were a real enemy soldier on whose information lives and victories actually depended. And as he listened, he felt within himself some dark brothering instinct that seemed almost to parallel that stream. On the instant, he grappled with it fiercely, but it was like trying to sieze vapor; the measured, conversational flow of the sergeant's voice as it swept calmly toward the promise of brutality was as hypnotic on Pendleton as on the prisoner. It was something more. It was provocative, sensual; a wind of sex swept through the private and he looked sharply back toward the other men. They seemed to feel nothing. Their heads were inclined politely toward each other, like the heads of gossiping women over a backyard fence.

"On the other hand," Cox was saying, "we have the hard way. The hard way is when you refuse to talk, and we—well, we make you talk. This way doesn't have very much to recommend it at all, since you end up in fairly poor shape, and we have the information anyhow. Now I know you're a rational man, and I'm confident you'll want to make it easy on all of us, so I'm not going to lecture you any further. You just take about ten seconds or so to make up your mind, and let me know how you want it."

"What are you, crazy?" the prisoner demanded. "This is just an exercise, Sergeant Cox. It's supposed to be run by the rules, and the rules say I don't have to give you anything but name, rank, service number and date of birth. Anyway," he added, as though he had already begun to forget it, "I'm dead."

"Let's make that five seconds," Cox said.

Pendleton glanced at him nervously.

"Hey, man, he's kidding, for Christ's sake, isn't he?"

"Yes," said Pendleton desperately, "he's kidding."

140

The prisoner began again, "This is just a goddam game, and I'm not supposed—"

Cox hit him very hard in the stomach. The man gagged sharply and doubled over, his bound hands flying up like an A from the small of his back. Cox pushed the prisoner to the ground. He said to Pendleton, "Give me your canteen and your cap."

"What are you going to do?" His voice sounded breathless, as though he were looking for a way to be shocked, pleading for an excuse to himself for his presence at this scene.

Cox did not miss the jittery tone. If he had not realized it before, he knew now that this was an extraordinary opportunity to carry the education of Private Pendleton a large step farther. He said swiftly:

"*Move!*"

Pendleton lifted off his helmet and liner and handed Cox the crumpled fatigue cap he was wearing underneath them. He unsnapped the canteen case and pulled the olive plastic container free.

The prisoner was still wheezing and gasping for breath. Before he could catch it, Cox put the cap over his mouth and nose, pushing as much loose cloth as possible tightly between the man's teeth. He unscrewed the canteen and began pouring water over the cap in a rich stream.

"Jesus Christ, sergeant, you'll drown him!"

"No," Cox said. "No, I think he'll probably talk before it goes that far. If he doesn't, you'll just have to get me another prisoner." He poured another splash of water over the cap and held it tightly. The man was struggling wildly. Only after about fifteen or twenty seconds did Cox lift the cloth away.

Pendleton watched, fascinated, as the prisoner tried to recover. The man's face was white, mottled with red, as though murdering thumbs and fingers had ravaged his features from forehead to

141

throat. His rimmed, suffering eyes had room to express little beyond the shock of what was happening to him, the sense of having critically misjudged his part in a play that had suddenly flowed off the stage and into the audience. And was he still an actor, or had he become a spectator at his own mistake?

Pendleton tensed as he watched the man fight for breath. And then, with a stab of horror, he saw Sergeant Cox upend the canteen over the man's jammed mouth again.

He started to move. Surely, damn the consequence, surely he would strike out, knock the canteen away, let the heritage of gentle breeding express its indignation at this excess of realism. But the knowledge that it *was* realism—that Cox was acting in terms of a sense of reality somehow superior to his own—tangled the private's motions in a web of doubt. He was left with his body in an awkward stance, his open hand falling feebly back to his belt (for, much as a cat licks its privates when embarrassed, a man will always touch his belt when he has begun a move and decided against it); and his eyes locked briefly with the sergeant's in the first of what was to be two critically charged glances between them, the other coming later in the day, before their respective "deaths" in the mock conflict that lay ahead. And Pendleton said nothing, did nothing, as Cox finished his work.

"What say, friend? You want to talk now?"

It was several more seconds before the man could speak. When he could, he said, "Hell, yes, I'll talk. You think I'm going to let myself get maybe drownt playing war?"

"This must be a friend of yours, Pendleton," Cox said. "He thinks this is play."

"It's a war game, sergeant," Pendleton said heavily. "It's a war *game*."

"Yes," Cox said, "a lot does depend on where you put the emphasis." He helped the prisoner sit up. "Get started, son."

When the man was finished, Cox said, "Right, thank you. I'll carry this to Sergeant Sherman. Pendleton, take this man to the POW area. You can untie him when you get him there."

"Yes, sergeant." He stood up and helped the prisoner up. Cox still sat in the grass, smoking serenely, like a poet on a hill.

"Pendleton," Cox said.

"Yes, sergeant."

"Remember what I told you. Remember where you are."

"Yes, sergeant."

"You're here."

In the makeshift prisoners' compound, the dead Aggressor was playing solitaire. He glanced up as Pendleton came in with the prisoner.

"Mother*fuck*—what happened to *you?*"

"These guys have got a Gestapo agent in camp," the prisoner said, "and the dogsucker tried to kill me. He really did, you know," he said to Pendleton.

"I know."

"Did you talk?" the dead Aggressor asked.

"Fuckin'-A-well-told."

"Traitorous pig. I would have been faithful unto death if I weren't already dead."

"You think it's a joke? You tell him," he said to Pendleton.

Pendleton was untying him. "It's no joke," he said.

"Fuckin'-A."

"Listen," the dead Aggressor said, "you guys be careful with those goddam blanks. They hurt."

Pendleton walked slowly back to the Company area. He thought: *You stood by and watched a man—don't temporize— tortured. And you were indignant, and you thought all the right thoughts, and you did nothing. Which, as somebody somewhere is supposed to have said once, is the only prerequisite for the triumph of evil. Doing nothing. And not only that. Somewhere*

143

inside yourself, in some way curiously connected with the struc-
ture, tastes and habits of your swingin' dick, you liked it.

Except that perhaps it wasn't evil at all. Perhaps Cox was a good man. Doing something. Behind him, he heard the two captive Aggressors, dead and damaged, begin a game of blackjack on the hard bare dirt floor of their compound. One, then both, commenced a mocking snatch of song, a marching song sung out of motion, almost lost in the clatter of the Company readying itself for battle.

> If I die in a combat zone
> Put me in a box and ship me home
> Fold my arms across my chest
> Tell my girl I've done my best—

And, almost affectionately, the coda.

EIGHT

AT 1730 the Company called in again.

Track had been banking the waning fire of his Benzedrine with cup after cup of coffee, now cold and overstrong; the porcelain was speckled with grounds, and his thoracic nervous system was starting to pick up the bill. His gut hurt in a neat little semicircle deep inside, just above his navel. When the radio kicked in, he was going over his figures again; soon things would be moving so fast he would have to have most of the equations instantaneously available in his mind.

Soon was now.

"Vulcan one, this is vulcan two, vulcan one, this is vulcan two. How do you hear me? Over."

Track pushed in the push-to-talk button on the side of his small square black microphone. "Vulcan two, this is vulcan one. I hear you five by. Over."

"Vulcan one, sitrep follows. Please stand by. Over."

"Vulcan two, authenticate six Romeo. Over."

There was a pause. "Vulcan one, I authenticate six Romeo as November November. Over."

"Vulcan two, confirmed. Standing by for your report. Over."

Some dryness frosted the lieutenant's body in a fall replica of

147

sweat. He shifted in his chair. The bony lights of the room hammered on his weariness.

"Vulcan one, here is sitrep. All information follows from outlaw interrogation and patrol observation. Aggressor Force in one-half company strength occupies position on map coordinates delta niner mike seven. Repeat, delta niner mike seven. Defensive posture maximal, armament limited to automatic weapons and light mortars. Details follow." Track noted them rapidly on the pad before him. Sherman was thorough and exact. His information did not require elaboration. "Position is further described as unwooded plateau, seven hundred meters in width on three sides, approached by wooded slopes at an angle of fifteen to eighteen degrees, five hundred meters on the fourth side, approached from the river by cliff, maximum incline of fifty degrees. Are you hearing? Over."

"Vulcan two, I am hearing you five by. Your information is excellent. What is your own status? Over."

"Vulcan one, we are ready to go. Over." Sherman's voice seemed to have summoned some urgency in the ear of the tin room of the static-ridden radio.

"Vulcan two, stand by for my orders. Out."

Track began to work. Aggressor Force held its position strongly, but without great imagination. According to his information, two of the slopes provided fields of fire so clear that an assault on them would have to be diversionary. The third offered better cover all the way up to the enemy lines. The river side was apparently virtually unguarded. Track was already sure of how he would handle it, which meant that Sherman was unquestionably surer still. The computer would probably do no more than confirm them; Sherman would be chafing, restless; but that was the name of the game.

Track realized he was in combat. He looked around his office. It looked the same.

148

He went to the terminal and fed in his information. Real-time, on-line, no legs in this outfit—the computer delivered its analysis in eleven seconds. Track called the Company. The ritual of authentication took longer than the formation of the battle plan.

"Vulcan two, your orders follow. You will utilize maximum security in accomplishing encirclement of Aggressor position by all elements. You will feint in squad strength on the river approach at your time designated X. At X plus ninety seconds, you will feint in squad strength on the southern approach. At X plus one hundred eighty seconds, you will assault the western approach in full strength. This position is to be taken at any cost. Incidentally, it won't be very high. Your projected probable casualties, KIA and wounded are under thirty percent." They would have been less except for the fact that the second feint would send an entire squad into an exposed area where it could expect almost one hundred percent casualties. "Are you hearing? Over."

"Vulcan one, got you. Over."

"Vulcan two, get back to me when action is initiated and maintain open radio contact thereafter. Report progress and all modifications. And good luck." He paused. "Sergeant Sherman, I want Sergeant Melton's ass handed to him. Over."

"Roger wilco. Out."

Track replaced the microphone. Some system of energy seemed to brighten within him, making him briefly more luminous in his own view. His weariness, then, had been partly a function of a final thread of uncertainty, and now that was gone, gone in the calm rapid response of the computer, gone in the assurance that his company, his Company, would perform its ancient savage chore under a new authority whose measuring ways all but guaranteed the victory.

The command post of the captain of Aggressors offered first itself and then its burden of *déjà vu*. Melton, standing apart from

149

the misshapen circle of junior NCOs who were his staff, as though their company too far qualified the privacy of his command, noticed the sheltered bunker at the crest of the low hill that crowned his position—a cold dusty rectangle of discolored concrete still spotted with the debris of earlier playful wars: scraps of tarpaulin and plastic ground cover, a torn corner of clear overlay from a map case, the rusted ring of a smoke grenade.

The bunker offered an unobstructed view down to the winter-stiff fringe of naked trees splashed through with evergreen that fell to the east, west and south of the plateau. The river, its slow voice audible under the small cliff, was at his back. Melton stepped down into the bunker. Loose planets of gravel and concrete crunched under his cold boots. It was then—it was the view from there, standing in the embrace of the bunker—that his field of vision tricked him into the past.

He identified the duplication so swiftly that the instant missed all magic. It had been in southern Italy, in 1944, that he had surveyed an identical scene. That, too, had been before a battle, but a battle in which men died, and in which he had himself been wounded. There had been the same cold, the same unreasoning calm, the same barrenness of prospect that erased all sense of locale. That too had been a scene where the geography was little more than its own geology.

He stamped his boots to warm his feet. He knew, with irritation, that the cold—which was no more than normally intense for an ungracious middle-Atlantic fall—had affected him more than it had the younger men. Christ, he could hardly even see his breath, so it couldn't be bad. But under the black leather, the cold lay over his feet in layers as even as an extra pair of socks.

He signaled his second in command, who came over at the double with his right hand tacked to his helmet.

"Sergeant Rellin, we'll set up the CP here."

"Yes, sir."

150

"Take care of it."

"Yes, sir."

"And take charge of deploying the troops. If you can't cover a position this simple, and make it bulletproof in fifteen minutes, we'll give you back to the American Army."

The black sergeant grinned. Melton would handle this business with a precise combination of irony and expertise.

"I'd concentrate on the south and west flanks. But don't neglect the river altogether. That lieutenant may have a friend who has a submarine."

"Roger that, top."

"Captain."

"Sir!"

Melton could have been a captain, and if he had been, it was not improbable that he would have been a brigadier general by now. They had tried to make him an officer twice, once during the drive through Italy and then again in 1950, in Korea. But he had not wanted a commission. On both occasions he had examined his motives as closely as possible to be sure he was not indulging some callow aversion to the officer corps, some romantic attachment to his stripes—"Don't call me *sir*, son, I work for a livin'." He concluded he was not. There were sound enough reasons: apprehension of a postwar reduction in force, conviction that, as first sergeant of an infantry company, he already *was* where the power was: the last step authority might take before paper work sapped it of virility. A questionable thesis; ask any second lieutenant. But his own.

Rellin saluted and departed at the double. Melton rested his elbows on the parapet of the empty bunker—which would, in another few minutes, be the center of a flurry of men bearing radios, map cases, canteens of just-warm black coffee—and focused his field glasses on the outer perimeters of his position.

Already there was activity there. Into the open ring of magnifica-

151

tion at the center of darkness, tableaus leaped, and shifted with his scan: the back and shoulders of a soldier, the muzzle of a machine gun, the stubby stovepipe of a mortar, all collected by the glass. It was not so different from the Italian view. In the weapons there was perhaps a disquieting hint of modernity—it had struck the sergeant before that the new rifles and machine guns had an eerie futuristic look about them, as though they might squirt magenta death rays instead of bullets. In combat photographs from Vietnam, it was always the weapons Melton noticed, and they seemed out of place. The men—their uniforms, their poses, their faces swept with fear or fatigue—might have been from any one of the many episodes in this century of total war; but the black plastic bristle of the guns belonged in the next.

Melton dropped the glasses carefully back into their case and thought about Italy. That had been a very expensive year for him. He had lost friends, he had been in unsuccessful parts of successful operations under mishandled commands, he had been hit not quite often enough to be good for a war-bond tour, he had made mistakes of his own that had killed people he had been playing five-card stud with for three years, he had felt his resources of judgment and nerve leave him and then return a dozen times, each time a little more ambiguously than before, so that his talent for soldiering grew ever more complex, a loss here and a gain there. Well, they had all been in botches, and lost friends, and been hit, and messed up, and suffered subtle losses. He had won things too, medals and such.

He brought himself back to thinking about his new enemy. That was what they were paying him for this year. But he found he could not think of his new enemy without thinking of the Second World War again. There had not been computers then, but there had been an unimaginably vast bureaucracy the young lieutenant would have felt at home in. There had been the same manswarm of secret weapons, rumored and real, that had spiced

152

this greatest global conflict with refinements of death hitherto unknown: jellied gases, luminescent rockets and red-winged tracer bullets, hissing supplies of disease that remained mercifully untapped. And the big one—the looming, lingering cloudfist that drew an instant oblivion for thousands from the heart of the sun and promised to visit its black power on the children's children of the foe. Melton shuddered, remembering how the news had reached him. He had been back in the ZI at last, training troops for the invasion of Japan that now would never have to come about. Relief had swept through the excited confusion of the post as clarification reached them of this inconceivable triumph. Melton had gone alone to the club and drunk himself into a trance, seized with a terror that vacillated between anguish and self-contempt. Never before had he known a fear whose roots he could not discover. With a revelation—new but never to leave him after—that alcohol was a mode of philosophical inquiry, he tried helplessly to find the fear inside the golden lake in his glass, but could not. But in the morning, with the start of the next duty day, the fear was gone. It had never returned.

On that day, Lieutenant Track had not yet been born.

Some hours later, word reached Melton that one of his outposts had been taken. He began to feel more interest, and take more pleasure, in the game. He realized that the force sent against him might be in the command of a callow officer driven by a strange idea, and yet still be staffed by soldiers.

The day had fallen into an elusive dark as the Company came into position for the attack. It was past twilight and the sun was gone, but its final rays, sundered by the sullen light of the risen moon, remained as hints and echoes in the air, leaving spaces of strange illumination. The trees and their shadows presented a textbook problem of appearance and reality. The river was splattered with cold mist and sparkling silver around the gray rocks it fed on, but moved deep and blue against its banks. Judgment of distances was a matter of utmost delicacy.

Now as the forces prepared to close, the unreality of their setting penetrated the manner of their acts. Aggressor, haughty and secure on its moderate hill, lit cigarettes like tiny orange stars and talked among itself in more than whispers. On its perimeter, guards and outposts felt the presence of the Company with a palpable admixture of apprehension and indifference.

The Company, separating into its elements and moving through the darkness with a stealth too successful to be quite plausible, prepared for battle with a humorous air—and yet not altogether humorous. It did not take the exercise seriously, because to do so would be to take the Army seriously, and that—for a draftee—effects an intolerable loss of self. But it was impossible to be altogether light: armed men moving through silence and darkness toward a model of confrontation cannot manage a pure self-mockery. Somewhere in the Company was a dim, rising, inarticulable sense that it was occupied at last with the center of soldiering; for if armies out of battle spend all their weary days performing or avoiding an infinity of mild minor degrading chores and labors, some purpose comes into them when they prepare to kill. It has no reference in patriotism or sense of cause, but in something deeper and more singular, and each man in the field that night was touched by a sense of it.

For Cox, it took the form of a rill of pure incoherent joy, and the joy turned into a feeling for his men that he might have recognized, had he been over twenty, as affection. Instead, it translated itself into a renewed lust for fluid order, for command, control, for watchfulness, for staying close and careful.

He had his orders, and he liked them, and disliked himself for liking them. To his squad had gone the role that was purest melodrama, though not all of them were precisely aware of that.

154

In the next half hour, he would almost certainly die at the head of his men, and with equal certainty, few of them would survive him. He was sorry in a way that he was not to be an instrument of the final logic of the action: splattered with red plastic and tagged by an umpire, he would sit on the sidelines being dead while the Company overran their deluded foe, divided by simple movements and ultimate sacrifices; and he would have half preferred to be the platoon leader who would release the final sweep and watch its deadly order bring the formal triumph. But with an even greater intensity, there had been triggered in him a remote warm pleasure at the idea of an empty gesture on an open field. Perhaps it was Sherman's sense of that that had chosen him; more likely it was chance, more likely it was where Cox had been standing in the little circle of men; or a slow rumination over the alphabet; or simply—nothing. Sherman had, in any case, looked closely at the younger sergeant as he put out the word.

". . . That's how the computer calls it, and that's how we play it."

"Did we need a computer to tell us that? Christ!"

"That's not the point," Sherman said patiently.

"It's obvious."

"Well, I don't care why you do it. You can do it because it's what you or I or any halfway intelligent leader of troops would do, or you can do it because the computer said do it. Any way you like. Sergeant Iacone, your platoon—and otherwise unassigned elements of Sergeant Cox's platoon—will come in and mop up from the western side. Sergeant Cox, you will designate one squad to mount the opening diversion from the river and another to come up from the south—here. The rest of your people will provide cover fire and support for the third platoon. Questions."

"Yeah," said Cox. "That southern side has got the longest exposure, the least cover and the best fire lanes for them. Right?"

"Right."

155

"So I gather we aren't worried too much about how much luck we have there."

"The lieutenant says to expect close to one hundred percent casualties," Sherman said impassively.

Iacone snickered. "Jesus, Billy, you'll love that. It's a real John Wayne ride."

"The lieutenant says the computer says we should be able to do the job with no more than thirty percent casualties," Sherman said, "and that ain't bad."

"No, it's not. Did he need a computer to tell him that?"

"He needs a computer to tell him when to wipe his ass," Iacone said.

"And where to put the paper."

"Knock off. Get back to your people and get them together."

"*Ja wohl*, baby."

"Hey, how do we get up the river?"

"With a boat," Sherman said.

They had a boat: an inflatable black rubber raft big enough to hold six men and their gear. It was inflated by CO_2 cartridges, but there weren't any, so Young and the other men in his squad were taking turns blowing it up with a foot pump.

"This is gonna be an all-night job," one of them whispered.

"Just blow the fucker up enough so she'll float," Young said, "and keep quiet."

"If you call this thing *she* you must be a real boat freak," the man said.

Young glanced at his watch. The Company was going to start raining death and destruction on Aggressor in a very few more minutes, and when that happened, he and his makeshift commandos were supposed to be on their way up the slope from the river. "All right, that'll do it." They pushed the raft into the river and struggled aboard.

156

"Hey, man, is this authentic? I mean, do infantry outfits usually carry around rubber boats as part of their gear?"

"We got this one from a partisan who was willing to risk his life to help us overthrow Hitler's hordes," Young explained. "He also had a beautiful olive-skinned sixteen-year-old daughter who was proud to do her bit for democracy."

"Did you say she bit it?"

"So that's where you were."

"I seem to still hear her tiny yelps of awakened passion."

"Brain, Igor, tonight we get brain."

"All right, now, shut the fuck up," Young whispered.

"You talked. Why can't we talk? You talked."

"I'm the boss."

"Dig it."

"Who's rowing?"

"Rowing? We're sinking."

"That's a forward motion," Young said. "We're just tilting a little."

"Tilt, no replay."

"Can you dig it?"

"Shut *up*."

The current had begun to do a better job than the oars. The men in the raft were half wet and already cold, and the mist and silence of the river chilled their conversation away altogether. Young checked his weapon and looked at his watch again.

For Pendleton, it took an infinitely more complicated form. Like most draftees, whose reliance on scorn makes it necessary that they judge professional soldiers by their lowest attributes, Pendleton could not imagine that Cox's visible pleasure in this foolish and ugly game came from anything more subtle than a killer instinct. It was the suggestion of that instinct in himself that troubled him so profoundly. It came, surely, from something he

157

was accustomed to be ruthless with, some atavism, some reluctant obeisance to warlike blood. He knew the craft of soldiering was one he could handle more comfortably now than he was willing to admit; knew Cox was not far from being pleased with him; and he hated that. No, used to hate it; now perhaps he only wanted to. The thing, the unman, that Cox had tried to make him, he was now not too far from being. It was so simple. Cox commanded respect; he was so superb at his job that ethical judgments on him were replaced by aesthetic satisfaction. It seemed that if you wore his uniform you had to emulate him, or the uniform would taunt you out of your defensive dislike and leave you empty. Trying to be like Cox would make you a monster, Pendleton thought wildly, but failing to try would leave you less than a man. He glanced over at Cox, but the sergeant had turned to the man at his left, and Pendleton could not see his face.

They were lying at the edge of the tree line. Before them stood the open slope which crested on the southern perimeter of the Aggressor plateau, barren and still in the blue moonlight. It seemed a short distance, but—once out of the cover of these trees—it was a distance that afforded no protection whatever from the two machine guns clearly visible on the ridge. In the clear quiet light, Pendleton thought he could see the red triangles taped to the gunners' helmets.

The enemy.

Well, holy fuck and wow.

More complicated. For his mockery was now something he had to search for. He had lost his pure, spiteful indifference to the Army: that, he realized, had happened when he began to perform duties he knew he should despise. And now there was—he could not help it—there was excitement in his spirit as he lay and waited.

"Hey," Pendleton whispered, "I can feel my heart beating against the pine-needle floor of the forest."

Cox turned to him patiently. The sergeant was a dark shape,

158

no more, in which two blue eyes glimmered like turquoise devil beads. He put his mouth against Pendleton's ear, and his whisper was less a voice than a vibration. "Move your squad at my signal. We'll drop grenades on them first; though there ain't much chance of taking out either of those positions that way from here. But the smoke'll cover you some. Stay spread out and keep your irons on rock-and-roll"—full automatic—"and don't stop shooting till you run out of bullets."

"Chances are—what?"

"Very, very damn slim. You know the story here, Pendleton." He pointed up the slope. "Those machine guns are fixed into overlapping trajectories that cover that area like a blanket. As long as they're both working, won't nothing move up there for long. That's what's called a killing zone."

Even now, Cox was the teacher. To Pendleton, a tantalizing connection then suggested itself, made a bid to tell him why he was becoming a proficient soldier. He dismissed it with that ready contempt we reserve for answers both facile and correct.

"If this was for real," he murmured, "I don't believe I'd go up that slope."

Cox moved his lips again, and Pendleton heard him say, "And if you refused, I would kill you. Because this is where discussion ends, young man."

And the attack began.

There were sounds of firing from the river, but the noise of the gunners on the slope clearing their weapons and letting the bolts fly home were louder. Then there were dry hollow swishes and clickings all through the trees, short chugging sounds, and sighs dropping through the uncharged air, and smoke bloomed in brief pillars up on the plateau. But still, strangely, there was more of silence in the night than of any other quality; and the men in the tree line to the south moved no more, and made no more noise, than as though the battle were still only an idea. Pendleton came

159

slowly to his hands and knees, as though to rise. Cox put his finger through the pin of a smoke grenade. Pendleton's squad began to shift and stir. He looked at them and thought, irony tinged with an unwelcome passion:

> O God of battles,
> Steel my soldiers' hearts—
> Possess them not with fear
> Lest the opposed numbers pluck their strength
> From them.

Cox's arm moved in the darkness. A tiny cylinder lifted into the sky. Still he did not shout, but touched Pendleton on the shoulder and said in a normal tone, "Get going."

In his office, the lieutenant waited for information.

Young's ship had come in, but not quite the way he had intended. Its seaworthy qualities had finally given over under too much weight and too little air and it expired just under the enemy guns; which, to be sure, weren't there. The computer had been right in suspecting there would be no defense by arms where the earth itself provided.

They scrambled up the steep incline, weapons at the port. They were still laughing at a joke someone had told earlier, and that was perhaps the first sign of its enemy Aggressor had. By the time Young's squad gained the edge of the ridge, it had opposition.

Here was no lack of cover, and most of them got to it in time. But two men died in a red plastic storm just beyond the ridge, and went down cursing and slapping at their bodies as though they had been hit by bees; but the others had good cover and concealment, and worked their way closer to the firing, guarding each other's moves in the swift progression they had learned on the close-combat course—and, miracle beyond telling, it seemed to work.

160

A plastic round scalded Young's cheek and an anger took him, identical in both quality and kind to the anger of a child hit by an iceball in a snowball fight. Unfairness spoke to him in a voice equal to danger's: it hurt, it could blind you, this was going too far. He was having a hard time finding targets, and the plastic was falling around him like the patter of rain on compost. He fired short bursts in the direction of the enemy, frustrated. Then the flooding false reality of the scene shattered totally as an officer, a captain, came to ground beside him, flashing on his arm a band with a huge red luminous E. An umpire, an evaluator.

"I think you're dead, trooper."

"Just a flesh wound, sir. I can make it," Young said bravely.

"Turn your head. Nope, that's straight on. You've got a bullet in the brain, pal."

"No wonder my reflexes are slowed."

"Get over there, troop. You men too."

"Christ, isn't there anybody left? That sure was quick." But the firing had not stopped. Young touched his cheek. The plastic was darkening and hardening; he could almost peel it off. It would probably leave a hell of a bruise.

The machine guns opened fire.

Cox's grenade had landed below them and the smoke was pouring into the position. Their firing began a little low, and then came slowly up, starting the crisscross from which there could be no refuge. But the smoke gave some cover; if it made the gunners uncertain, if it somehow confused them out of their methodical interdiction, there might be spaces to move through, there might be men of Pendleton's squad who would be left to take the objective.

The squad had moved out fast and deployed nicely. They were shouting, and firing steadily, tiny fountains of spent brass from

161

their jumping probing weapons rising over their shoulders into the light.

Cox's reserve squad was putting down a high cover fire, but the sergeant himself, having thrown his grenade, felt a sudden momentary lassitude, as though his adrenalin had been dammed and sent off somewhere that found its energy irrelevant. He rested his head briefly on his forearm, and in the full dark of his mind listened to the bogus bullets whip and whicker into the earth and leaves.

Clip into the leaves and trees.

Whine away.

And then the authenticity of the sound, the sound alone, came to him, and he snapped his head up. The difference was close to imperceptible, but he heard it. He did not even see the two men on the hill, stiff and prone and rolling. He said softly, "Sweet Jesus . . ."

He said, "Cease fire . . . *cease fire!* . . . CEASE FIRE!"

His own men heard him and—a little puzzled—stopped shooting. Their plastic rifles raised, they fired no more plastic bullets. But the gunners on the ridge continued to fire.

In his office, the lieutenant waited for information.

It's so real, ain't it grand? Did the man think that? He was running to the left of Pendleton and just behind him. Iron fingers of the cold earth were spouting in terraced rows all about him. He ran with his head and helmet low, for there was no doubt these things could make a mess of your eyes if one caught you there.

One caught him there anyway. It tore through his skull, freeing the constants of his brain, shattering and scattering everything and keeping it within the containing well of the helmet. The man was lifted, twisted, flung down, dropped, left behind.

162

Pendleton made it less than halfway up the hill. It may be that he had time to lock eyes briefly with Cox—certainly his head was turned that way, he saw him—as the sergeant ran past him. There was perhaps time for an easing of the puzzle, a message between them. But then Cox was gone into the thinning smoke, his face painted with the cool white of the moon, his voice trailing behind him like the printed words of a comic balloon: ". . . down, hit it, down . . .": that was no doubt what he wanted to say, meant to say, but it is more likely he was shouting obscenities, or simply shouting. His bayonet was fixed to the muzzle of his rifle. It too bore strokes from the dim palette of the dark light.

Pendleton paused at the sight.

A wall of ice smashed into his legs and he fell heavily. Cursing. Numbed by it. On his knees, he was hit again.

Cox ran. But why was he running so slowly and thinking so clearly? Did he, finally, himself, think—or know—that this exercise was just a joke? But he had recently told Pendleton that this was where discussion stopped. Then surely that meant that discussion stopped inside your own head, that above all. *Hit.* That was easy, he could go through that forever. *Hit.* Mateland had wanted a lot of discussion. He was a talking soldier. Cox had found him—still in uniform, for God's sake!—in a bar in town, and brought him back to be killed. He had run from his little crime, tried to run into the healing glare of the summer sun itself, and the scared young guard had shot him, and, Jesus, a .45 will put a hole in you, a hole to see through or dance through. . . . Mateland had wanted to talk, so Cox sat with him for almost an hour in that smoky purple bar, getting stains on his clean sharp well-turned immaculate uniform from sloshing pitchers of beer, until it became clear that Mateland only wanted to argue and finally to beg. That desperation turned him back into a thief and a deserter, so Cox

163

simply took him back the hard way. The Army, the real Army, was always the hard way; that was why it was so clean. Some men, most men, never understood that; some—Pendleton— resisted but could be taught. You had only to wake up an old dream in their blood. It had nothing to do with the flag, *hit*, but it did have something to do with the uniform. And *hit*. And that was the big one, Cox thought importantly, swelled with the pride of his death: that one had a different flavor altogether from the others. That was why Cox always kept his uniforms neat and creased. And very clean.

He had been hit four times by the gunner who was still firing when he reached him. Mr. Track's computer had provided an unbeatable realism which had gone into his belly, and one bit of the realism had ruined his left arm, taken it out altogether. So it was with the rifle in one hand that he came over the barrel, calmly, indifferently, almost sweetly, and with practiced smoothness and precision slid the bayonet into the boy's chest, up to the hilt, not seeing the frightened and finally knowing face glance down into the explosion of blood as cloth and skin and muscle and then bone gave way to the rushing pouring steel. Cox's finger jerked on the trigger and a short stream of plastic bullets squirted into the open wound, splashed hot into the welling lake of blood. The sergeant and the private fell together behind the finally silent gun.

And in his office, the lieutenant waits for information.

Pendleton thought that they had moved him down under the trees, because the ground no longer seemed to slope, and he was almost comfortable. But they had not. The medic had jammed a needle into his upper leg, and with the advent of its kind juices the voices and faces of the men around him began to recede and lose their interest.

164

He wanted his girl, and spoke her name. That brought her to him, and he marveled that he had never thought of it before. She knelt by him, more slender and delicate even than he had remembered, the light of other suns playing through her hair. He thought perhaps she was nude, although somehow he could not see her clearly enough to tell. She was kneeling by his open thighs and looking up into his face with a sweet quizzical smile. After a while that began to irritate him, because what he really wanted was for her to blow him, and she just kept looking at him as though she hoped to change his urgency into something vague and tranquil, answerable by a charged exchange of glances.

He tried to raise his head and she said, as though to someone else, in a rough male voice, "No, Jesus, don't let him look at it." He lay back.

She left. He thought of food.

He played with his toy soldiers. They were of metal and plastic, they fell locked into the same positions they had stood in. Their battles were tremendous, they contested forts and tables and boxes, there was a fire in a burning hymn into the sky of the room, he was heartily sorry for his manifold sins and wickednesses, but she would have mercy on him—

—burning him—

It started coming back. He said, "*Jesus.*"

It'll be OK. Hold on.

"Give me another shot of that shit, for God's sake, please, hurry, *please.*"

"Can't, dammit." *Can't.* "Too dangerous."

Dangerous.

"Jesus God, *please!*"

Can't.

"All right," Pendleton said. "OK, it's all right." He tried to lift his head again, and let it drop back again. He looked up into the black center of the room of the earth until he caught

165

sight of the point of light at the center of the center. And then the real thing—the final mission of the infantry—presented itself to him, and he performed it.

Track, through Major Haslip, had gotten hold of a helicopter, and the two officers dropped into the area ten minutes later. Track had never been in a helicopter before. It was strange and exciting to him. They were so low, so open. The lights of the post went swarming by underneath them as though the earth and its burden had been flattened and poured onto a swift conveyor belt; and the darkness of the fields and hills came pouring after the lingering forlorn yellow dashes of the outbuildings after which the post unfolded into the golf course, the woods, and there were the greater lights, in the gay operatic colors, of the Air Force base, and then more darkness, broken now only by shapes and masses of lighter tones of itself.

And they were there so swiftly! The pilot, a warrant officer with a monumental red moustache, set the helicopter down in the very center of the plateau. Track could even see the white faces of the men below grow larger and move away from him, and dry leaves and dirt and bits of trash and fabric rose in a vortex to greet the whirling rotor. He bent double getting out of the helicopter and carefully stayed bent double getting away from it.

Major Haslip had spoken to him only once during the flight.

Track found First Sergeant Melton outside his command post, speaking quietly to Sergeant Iacone. He did not salute, but he turned to the officer at once. Track looked at his face and then glanced away and did not look again.

"What happened?"

"We were issued two cases of live ammunition." Melton said flatly. "It went to the perimeter machine guns on the south flank."

"What casualties?"

166

"Five killed, three wounded, one critically."

"Dear God."

Melton started to weep. "Sergeant Cox tried to—excuse me, sir—"

Track turned blindly away. He saw Major Haslip begin to talk to one of the umpires, a tall thin captain who was tapping his pencil rhythmically against his clipboard. He walked past them toward the southern slope, looking for his men. But Death, who turns men into scenery, had been there before him.

NINE

"TALK ABOUT the—uh—'profession of arms,' the 'final gift'—like it was—excuse me, as though it was— were—a *present*—that's all no damn good at this point, it sounds like lies. Worse, it sounds like truth. Excuse me."

See Track now. He is a little, not very, drunk. The officer across the table, slender and with the face of an astronomer, is in uniform, but the lieutenant is wearing a suit. Although he is a soldier only experimentally, Track appears costumed when he is in civilian clothes. His hair is clipped so closely, and the teardrop-shaped wire-rimmed thick glasses look like the goggles of a motorcycle policeman from Los Angeles. But he is strikingly well dressed, nothing of the short-sleeved see-through shirts of the Pentagon. His suit is a bespoke medium-gray herringbone, beautifully cut and obviously expensive. His shirt is very heavy pink broadcloth, his tie is a wide regimental silk echoed by a pocket square. To see him thus is to feel freshly the power clothes have in putting parameters to personality. He is so strikingly turned out as to make the senior officer who is his dinner partner almost uneasy without knowing quite why.

They are waiting for their food. Captain Page is drinking dark draft beer and the lieutenant is drinking brandy and water. The

171

officers' club is almost as opulent as an officers' club in Germany or Japan. The walls bear bad oils and tapestries, the table linen is snowy, indeed a snow field, subdued light sparkles from wineglasses and silver, pulling ruby flashes from burgundy tones, metal spears of light. The men are waiting for fresh brook trout and a bottle of Moselle, but it may happen that they—or, at any rate, Lieutenant Track—will be somewhat disoriented with drink by the time the food arrives.

For Page, this dinner has the mood of a business engagement. He all but explicitly feels they should wait until coffee before they talk about these things. But that is obviously impossible. Track is too stunned, even now, and will talk of nothing else. In any case, Page is curious, technically curious. He would like to get the lieutenant away from these general considerations, which, he reflects, seem to have crept into Track's mind and ruptured the clarity and order that must have prevailed there. Page does not want to talk about the profession of arms, which is not his true profession despite the uniform on his back and the bars on his shoulders. He is willing to be sympathetic, he would be less than human otherwise, indeed he is truly sorry and shocked. But he wants to know *what happened*. Track shifts abruptly:

"I'll be court-martialed, of course."

It seems likely. "Well," Captain Page says cautiously, "perhaps not even that. Some inquiry, obviously, something will have to be done, God knows your program is going to be badly chewed up by red tape teeth before anything else can be done with it. But—"

"It doesn't matter. All that matters is that they understand it was *my* error, human error, operator error. The idea is sound."

Page sucks at his glass. "No one disputes that."

"Oh, hell, Charlie!"

"Well—"

"I still can't believe it."

172

"And I'm still not totally clear about it. What it seems to go back to is that you didn't define a work area in your program as being set to zero initially, right?"

"Yes. I just—excuse me—reserved storage for it."

"Then you had no way to predict the contents."

"I had no way to predict the contents," Track repeats slowly. "Yes. That is correct." He signals a waiter, who swims noiselessly into his vision over the carpet. "One more. You?"

"No. Thanks. But why?"

"Well, I clear storage in my partition every time I finish a program—"

"And you assume everybody else has habits just as good. How'd you catch it?"

Track shrugs impatiently. "I went over every step and ran into the problems of too little storage again. So I checked out the whole contents of the core."

"And?"

"There it was."

Two figures had matched up on a sheet of paper, giving the exact federal stock number of the ammunition wrongly ordered. Page wonders how Track felt, looking at those numbers. The simplicity of the mistake is awesome. He suddenly becomes accessible to the vagrant seed of pity that has been trying to surface through his professional concern, and wishes to say no more, but Track is dully going through it again, as though repetition might force some alteration on the past.

"I was feeding in data on the munitions-supply distribution, and the computer rejected a command—flagged it as a violation of storage protection. I remember how pissed off I was at having to restart that whole section of the program. So I just typed in the master code to get access to all core storage—I modified that section of the supervisor myself, you know—then I reentered the data and went on from there. Smooth as silk. Smooth as silk because I

173

picked up data from a partition that had been used in an exercise by the ordnance supply people at the other new terminal. Picked it up and added it to my own field. You don't want another?"

"No. Really. I—I wish I knew what the hell to say."

Their waiter arrives with dinner. Halfway through the silent meal, Page looks up from his plate, he is almost smiling, and says: "— except sorry about that. And be more careful next time."

Bureaucracy is not responsive to drama, at least not until drama has aged into history. So only an overorganized and poetic mind could find irony in the fact that, on Tuesday morning, orders were received in the company promoting Track to captain and Pendleton to private first class. First Sergeant Melton had such a mind. When the papers crossed his desk, he stared at them dully for several seconds before breaking into his rich fat laugh.

Reynolds, already buried in the orderly room under the disposition forms of slaughter and mistake, heard the laugh, and was shocked. He was one of the college kids Melton made corporals, and he had a strongly developed sense of indignation over practically everything. It left no room for the idea that death leaves room for laughter. He stopped typing for a moment and swore softly, and thus having accomplished his duty toward his morality, began typing again, glancing toward the door occasionally as shadows passed it, for the lieutenant—the captain—had not yet come in. Reynolds wondered what he should say to him.

It had begun snowing sometime after midnight and stopped sometime before dawn—not a heavy snow, a sullen November flurry that had left mounds and streamers of white slush over the black iron of the ground. Reynolds thanked God that they weren't outdoors any longer; it was rotten weather to play soldier in. In the doorway behind him, he felt the presence of the first sergeant.

"Morning, top," he said again. He had said it when Melton

174

came in twenty minutes earlier, but the first sergeant had not seemed to hear. Now he said mildly, "Good morning, Reynolds. You made coffee yet?"

"Yes, sir, piping hot."

"If it's left over from yesterday morning, young specialist, your ass is mine."

Reynolds was hurt. "Would I do that?"

"You would. You have. You are the only company clerk in this battalion who uses the same grounds for a week. I should send you back to a rifle platoon."

"But I'm invaluable, top," Reynolds protested.

"You just go on believing that." Melton ran three inches of stale black coffee steaming into his chipped china mug. He leaned against a file cabinet and began sipping carefully. After a period of silence, Reynolds said, "What's going to happen, top?"

"Just do your typing. I've got more for you. You're going to have a very busy day."

"I knew some of those guys," Reynolds said.

"Yes, and you think that gives you some kind of personal claim against the captain, don't you? Jesus Christ. You kids. All you kids in the whole goddam Army today. You think there's something special about dying. Let me show you something. Come on, goddam it, get off your dead ass and come here with me." The clerk followed him into his office. "Look at that. What do you see?"

"Books," Reynolds said.

"Books, right. Field manuals, tech manuals, ARs, DA and DOD directives, and God knows what-all. Army books on everything from the psychological effect of paint colors to preparation of color slides for audiovisual displays. And somewhere in there is an MOS listing which tells you all the things a man can do in the Army, all the jobs the Army has. I think there are over three hundred. A man can be a clerk, like you are, or a superclerk, like I am.

175

Or then we have pastry cooks, generals' aides, newspapermen, air-conditioner experts, tugboat captains, fixed-winged aircraft repairmen and mechanics, TV announcers, instructors in urology or topography or counterintelligence, plumbers, electricians, dental surgeons, psychologists, blacksmiths, and several hundred more. But it's all, every bit of it, in aid of one thing only. Now look at this. What is it?"

"A bayonet," Reynolds said.

"That's right," said Melton. "Now you know. Now shut up and go back and do your work."

"Yes, first sergeant."

It was Cox's bayonet. The machine gunner's blood had been wiped from the edge of the blade, but some of it was still crusted into the guard, mixed with a hardened film of plastic. Melton put the bayonet down on top of his desk.

Track came in shortly after ten o'clock. He had been up at Battalion for two hours. His face was efficient and composed, the face of a man who had organized his damages and was dealing with them in his mind successfully. Melton handed him the promotion orders.

"Oh, Christ."

"Congratulations, sir."

"Yeah, sure. They'll tear these up soon enough."

Melton said nothing.

"Come into my office."

He closed the door behind them and went over and sat behind his desk. Melton had noticed before, with amusement, that the young officer invariably went to sit at his desk, fronted by his nameplate and flanked by his flags, whenever he felt the need for symbols to buttress his authority, which was usually. Melton was not amused now.

The office was unchanged since the day before. The field radio still perched massively on the captain's desk, and the surface beside

176

it was littered with scratch pads and flow-chart pads. The computer terminal stood in its corner like a criminal.

Track for a while conducted an intense study of the laces of his shoes. Finally he said, "I don't know why I feel the need to explain myself to you."

"I didn't ask you to. I don't want you to."

"Sit down, sergeant, will you?"

Melton sat.

"It's the center of a weapons system, sergeant, and it works. It didn't make any mistake. I did."

"Are you certain, sir?"

"I made a programming error."

"I thought you were such a hot-shit computer man."

"I am. I won't make that error again."

"How expensive will your next one be, sir?"

"Goddammit! I'm prepared for that. You should be too. You've seen men die before."

"I haven't seen lives wasted before."

"You don't know whether they were wasted or not. That's one of the things we can't ever know."

Melton said, "We?"

"What?"

" 'We?' "

"Look, I know what you think of me as a soldier, sergeant."

"I don't think anything of you as a soldier, captain. I don't think you are a soldier. I think you are a company commander who sat in his office and played with buttons while his men died."

Track said nothing.

"Sir," Melton went on, "one of those men who died *was* a soldier—"

"He was a soldier who would have been in a world of shit after what he did if he hadn't died doing it," Track said bluntly.

Melton stood up. He went to the window and opened the

blinds. In the brick barracks across the way, softened by its tracery of snow, he could see figures in the lighted rooms: the men of the company assembling their gear for the next formation.

"Captain—"

"He was insane, Larry. A savage. To try to stop it like that."

"No," said Melton, "he was just the man who picks up the bill. Now will you please get the Christ Almighty fuck out of here, captain, for the rest of the day, because I don't want to look at you, and there is so much work to do."

"Don't push your luck with me, sergeant!" Track flared.

"Please. I'm asking you. Begging you."

Track sighed. "I wonder how you would have handled it if you'd been a medieval archer and somebody stuck a crossbow in your hands."

"Please," Melton said again.

Melton stood by the window for a long time. In a few minutes, he saw Track, rendered shapeless inside the heavy overcoat with the silver bars glimmering on the shoulders in the pale fall snowy sun, get into his car. The top of the Corvette was in place, and the windows closed, but before the resonant buried voice of the motor took up, Melton heard a gentle snatch of song flash from its radio, overloud, and then die away as the captain touched the controls. Melton recognized the tune, tried to identify it, and could not. The Corvette trudged away through the snow. Without knowing why, the first sergeant, still holding his coffee cup, went to the other window, from which he could see the main gate of the post. He saw the captain's car slow down by the guard shack and saw the MP inside the shack throw a precise long-armed salute through the window. And he saw Track, inside his car, return it with a matching sharpness. Track, who usually saluted with all the class of a medical officer. Then the car pulled onto the highway and was gone, gone toward the city.

Melton went back to his own desk and lighted a cigar and took a drink from a small flat bottle of rye he kept in his middle drawer. He had a great many letters to construct. He started with one to the wife of one of the privates who had died on the hill, a man he did not know well at all. It would be easier that way. He would write last to Sergeant Cox's wife; perhaps by then he would be into the swing of his art and speak to her more beautifully. Not that she would care. But now only earlier phrases came into his mind, and he typed them mechanically. *It is with deep regret.* Deep, deep regret. Such deep regret. He found he felt no regret. *As your husband's commanding officer . . .*

He had been, of course, at his CP. Feeling able and assured, listening to the sounds of firing from the river and the trees. Mortars were dropping smoke shells, his men were running and holding and firing. It was a game, such a game, deep game. And he thought perhaps he could win it, could come up with responses that would end Track's dreams of mixed-media glory. Why had he not heard the different note in the machine guns? Cox had heard it. Why had he not? The light had been blue, dark, swarming and diffuse; it was a place for real killing and real dying; why had his intuition not given him that truth?

. . . a good soldier whose loss will be deeply felt. It was nothing less than a death in combat, though in a combat waged by ourselves against ourselves, to prepare us with the utmost rigor and reality for the defense of our land when the time comes and the chips are down . . .

Melton paused, because the melody from Track's radio was surfacing in his mind, and he wanted to name it. It mingled with others, then came clearer. Rock-and-roll, or what they now called just rock, the new music—he hated most of it—but he had heard before, and liked, this quiet tune: there it was: "Ruby Tuesday," by the Rolling Stones. A really beautiful song.

70 71 72 73 10 9 8 7 6 5 4 3 2 1